The Persian Lover
Creed and Greed

9-28-2025

Naser D. Shahrivar

Wishing you abundant happiness and success.

The Persian Lover
Creed and Greed
Shahrivar, Naser D.

ISBN: 978-0-9887077-3-3
Printed in the USA

Book Cover design by Naser Shahrivar

Inspired by the true story of a family and friends.
"I have risked my life by telling this story."
Naser

ACKNOWLEDGMENTS

I want to thank my wife, Patricia, for all her help and support. I would also like to thank my dear friends who offered their encouragement and support in helping me complete my book. My heartfelt gratitude goes to my editor, Lisa Gottschalk and Alexa Rose Pettinari, for their assistance, hard work, and dedication in helping me with editing my novel.

Sincere thanks to all my readers from the bottom of my heart.

Naser D. Shahriva

From left to right, Mikhail, Mami, Rayhan, Esrafil
This photo was taken one year before the death of Mami

What others are saying about: The Persian Lover/Creed and Greed

Dear Naser, I couldn't put your manuscript down; it really kept me engaged!
Lisa Gottschalk

"With the Iranian Revolution a: its backdrop, Shahrivar's
story illustrates the tenacity of lor and life against even the most devastating
political turmoil. Follow Babak through his tragic, but charming rustic
childhood and into the throes of :is thrilling, palpitating romances. This book
takes unexpected turns into seve-al different emotional arenas, making it an
engaging and surprising read, w:ch I greatly enjoyed."
Editor, Leah Lederman

"I am now through Chapter 2G. and I am loving Shahrivar's
story. ... A friend just asked m: what makes a good romance novel for a
woman. This chapter was excel:nt in describing a young man's first real sexual
relationship and his love for her Great chapter!
Editor, Michele Neville

"It is rare to discover a new au⁻or who's engrossing and entertaining at the
same time. I found this book tc be a page-turner; I waited with anticipation to
see what would happen next. Nost definitely a book you will not forget! It will
take you to a land where most :f us have never been or experienced the
hardships of government contro: We see a glimpse of personal lives greatly
influenced by this."
Alice Roepke Vega

"I love a book that I can't pu: down – it fulfilled my expectations; you'll enjoy
the story.
Editor, Rae Ann Holub, Linn Newsletter

"While immersed in an inner struggle for success, Babak misses much of the romantic wonder throughout his everyday life, but in a time of Iranian political strife, he stands with old friends and new, summoning the courage to oust his country's oppressors. Babak's tale is disparaging at times, merciful at others, and in the end, a heartwarming story of growth, mistakes, and the eternal lesson that it's never too late to discover what you've missed. I enjoyed it and I think you will too."
Editor & Novelist, Weston Kincade—WAKE Editing

"This story is a visceral and evocative journey into a part of history that has long been overlooked. Through its vivid storytelling, it brings to life experiences that have remained untold, shedding light on stories that demand to be remembered. It is both powerful and necessary, leaving a lasting impression on the reader. "
Editor & Writer, Alexa Rose Pettinari – Rose English Services

Biography

Naser D. Shahrivar was born in Tehran, Iran. As a child, he had a passion for art, writing, and storytelling, and dreamed of becoming an artist. His parents did not support his desire, thus forcing him to paint and write in secrecy. As a young adolescent, he used raw materials and dyes to mix his paint. He loved following his uncle into tea houses to sit and listen to the stories. As a youth, Naser won first place in the local Tehran competition with his painting and later advanced to the national competition. His high school play was featured on local television.

As a young man, Naser came to the United States, where he pursued studies in architecture and engineering. Disappointed in the program, he switched his degree to graphic and fine arts, earning a bachelor's degree in graphic design and fine arts. He began doing freelance artwork and teaching part-time art classes. Naser has been involved in the "art scene" for over 40 years before trying his hand at writing.

Naser has received many awards for his artwork. His most recent achievement was in the New York Nil Gallery's 5th Annual International Online Exhibit/Art Competition, where his painting "Frappent" received the Best Visual Artist Award. In 2021, His painting titled "Conversion" received the BEST PAINTING AWARD from the New York Nil International Online Exhibit/Art Competition. Naser's oil painting titled "Morning Calm" was selected as a finalist in the International Artist Magazine Competition and featured in that magazine's February/March issue.

Since 2012, Naser has devoted more of his time to art and writing. His first novel, "The Persian Lover," was published in 2017 and offered as an e-book on Amazon Kindle, earning rave reviews and perfect 5-star ratings. He has been diligently working on adapting it into a screenplay and is hopeful to see his story on the big screen. He has finished the screenplay and has entered many screenplay competitions.

2019 "The Persian Lover/Creed & Greed" was selected as a semifinalist in the Los Angeles International Screenplay Awards.

2021 "The Persian Lover/Creed & Greed" was selected as a finalist in the Creative Worlds Awards Screenplay Competition.

December 2021 "The Persian Lover/Creed & Greed" was selected as a finalist in the 7th Annual International Screenplay Comp.

Jan 2023 "The Persian Lover/Creed & Greed" was selected to be in The International London Lift-Off Film Festival Awards.

December 2024 "The Persian Lover/Creed & Greed" was selected as a finalist of the Villa de Rota Writing Film Festival of Spain, and "The Call of Evil" was selected as a semi-finalist, earning a $500 prize.

December 2024 "The Persian Lover/Creed & Greed" was selected by the Los Angeles International Screenplay Competition Diversity Initiative and received Quarter Finalist status, which placed his Screenplay on the Red List to be viewed by those in the industry. His works are collected throughout the country and abroad.

Table of Contents

Prelude
Once Haven

Since 2017, when this book was first published, the crises in Iran and the Middle East have been worsening daily. After the Islamic takeover of Iran living there has been hell for most people. More often these days, Iran is called a country of torturing, raping, and killing innocents. Iran is number one in the world for executions; we will talk about this later.

***

I have been thinking and contemplating rewriting this story once again. However, I am sure that writing this book could cost my life. What I mean is Iran's government could hire anyone, from anywhere around the world, to kill me or kill anyone who is against their regime. They also kidnap people in different countries and put them on a plane and take them to Iran to be executed.

***

September 16. 2022 will be a pivot day for the people of Iran. A new and unexpected revolution was escalated by the arrest of 22-year-old Mahsa for exposing part of her hair. The immoral Islamic government of Iran tortured and killed her within a few days of her arrest.

The school students, primarily teenage girls, initiated the uprising, and soon almost all schools throughout Iran followed this historic event.

The government's reaction was not something new. They shot, arrested, imprisoned, tortured, raped, and then killed the prisoners, including children.

This was not enough punishment for a person who chooses the kind of clothing she wants to wear or the right to wear her hair as she pleases. They remove the victim's organs and sell them to mostly European countries.

Nika, seventeen years old, is a girl with big dreams and hopes. She was the only child of the family. Nika hugged and kissed her father and her mother. "I love you," she told her parents. I am going to join my friends on the street who are demonstrating; this could be the last day of my life, she told her parents.

Her mother said. Please do not say such a thing, my dear Nika. You should eat something before you go.

I am hungry, but I will eat after I return. The innocent teen, with a heart full of love for people and Iran, goes to the streets of Tehran knowing that her fate could be death.

She never returned. She was arrested and was placed in a big cooler behind a delivery truck. She was raped and beaten with a baton, crushing her skull, and she was killed within a few hours of leaving her family. A few days later, her dead body was thrown on the street.

During the same uprising, Hasti, a fourteen-year-old girl abducted by the security forces, managed to escape a few times. Finally, she was arrested for the last time. Hasti was beaten with a baton by the security forces and taken to the hospital. Her skull was crushed, and her family was forced to confess that what happened to Hasti was not the government's doing; it was an accident.

Hasti was in a coma for months, and the doctors considered removing her from life support. Her family fought against it. Her mother sat beside her day and night, hoping that she would get better. Her father quit his job to be with her. The doctors did surgery without using an anesthetic, thinking that Hasti was going to die anyway. Finally, after months of being in a coma, she opened her eyes.

Today, she and her family live in Germany. She has lost almost all of her memories, but she can speak and still remembers Mahsa's name.

Many people have been and continue to be executed without a sentence or judgment. In 1999, over 1500 were killed in just three days.

***

"Raping the detained women before their execution is like going to Mecca. If the women are not to be executed, raping them is like going to Karbala," says the Islamic cleric of Iran.

The young boys were not excluded from rape, no end to the Islamic government of Iran's killing. No mercy is given for ten- or twelve-year-old children.

"Rape The Virgin," so they can't go to heaven after they die," said another Islamic cleric in Iran.

"Forty women do not have the brain of one chicken," said another cleric.

Under this religion, an innocent 9-year-old girl can be forced into marriage. A Muslim man could have many or temporary wives

Chapter 1

Wicked Games

It is the 1930s, Russia is in turmoil, war breaks out, and poverty follows.

The sickness is taking a toll on many people's lives. The citizens who have the means to do so leave the country. Countless people migrate to neighboring countries, including Iran. Mami (36) and his wife, Rayhan (33), have four boys. Their two youngest boys, Gabrielle (age 3) and Israel (age 1), died from sickness.

Mami, Rayhan, and their surviving two sons, Esrafil (5) and Mikhail (8), and Ghobad, Mami's brother (38), stand and weep over a newly prepared child-sized grave. Many other family mourners are present for their own loved ones' gravesites.

Mami, Rayhan, and their two sons, Mikhail and Esrafil, are on their journey back to their homeland, Iran. Mami worked as an engineer in Russia (Soviet Union). Ghobad joins the family.

Ghobad moved from Iran to Russia to live with Mami years ago, and now, because he has no other place to go, he relies on his brother's support. After much hardship and struggle, Mami hires a carriage to take the family to the border of Russia and Iran.

They are in the moving carriage cabin. Mami looks out, Rayhan weeps, and Mikhail sleeps between his mother and his father. Esrafil sleeps in the back seat, on one side of the luggage, and on the other side sits Ghobad, who is in thought, and peers out at the moonlit passing fields.

Within a year of their transition to the village of Shahrivar near Ardebil, Iran, Mami purchased a charming home. He travels to neighboring towns to repair motors and engines.

Mami plans to move to the big city of Tehran and work for the train companies, but his plan fell through. Suddenly, Mami was taken ill. While the family was hoping for his recovery, Mami's illness became worse day by day.

He spoke in broken words to his family, who surrounded him in his bed.

Rayhan holds Mami's hand, and Mikhail and Esrafil sit beside him, weeping. Ghobad sat there in thought.

Mami to Ghobad, "Please ensure that my family is cared for, and promise the children will continue their schooling. Do not sell any land or cattle. Be kind to the family and the workers. Feed the hungry people in the village.

"My dear Rayhan, I am so sad to leave you so soon with this sudden illness. I love you. When my boys get older, please tell them how much I love them." Rayhan kisses his hand, holds it on her chest, and weeps.

"Please do not speak of being gone. God forbid that. Do not worry, my dear brother, I will do everything you want me to do. I will take care of them as if they were my own family."

***

The village medicine man prescribed all the herbs he thought might help Mami, but none of them were effective in curing his illness.

For three nights, he told his family that he would die very soon.

Mami coughs and hears his family cry in the background of his brother's empty promises. He closes his eyes for the last time.

Mami's death left his wife, two sons, and all his property in the greedy hands of his brother.

Ghobad loved them for the inheritance. He forced the two boys to work on the farm and prevented them from attending school again.

He loved them only for their hard labor. As Mikhail grew older, his hatred towards Ghobad became increasingly obvious and intensified.

Chapter 2

Greed

Several years had passed. Ghobad and Rayhan were married, and they had their first son, Ali.

It was dark in the room, and Ghobad appeared with a lantern. He walked to sleeping Esrafil, who was now 12 years old.

Ghobad (uncle, stepfather) shook Esrafil.

"Wake up, Essy (short for Esrafil). It's time to go to the mill; you should arrive before others do."

Mikhail grunted. "Be careful, Father would never do this to you. If anyone gives you a hard time, let me know."

It was early morning, and dark out. Essy stood by a donkey with a load of grain on its back, and Essy held a stick.

"Essy, there's some bread, walnuts, dates, and water in this bag for you," said Ghobad. "Let me put this money bag around your neck, and when they pay you, put the money in it and don't tell or give the money to anyone."

12-year-old Esrafil yawned and replied, "Yes, uncle."

"Remember, do not ride the donkey on the way there."

"Okay, uncle."

It was noon, and Essy rode the donkey on his way home. He was passing through a small village close to his home.

He was eating bread, walnuts, and dates when three young boys appeared and stood in front of his donkey, blocking the road.

"Hey, boy, where are you going?"

"To Shahrivar," Essy answered.

"It looks like you went to the mill and sold your goods. If you give us some money, we will let you go." The boy in a striped shirt said.

"I don't have any money, so get out of my way."

Essy shook his stick in the air.

Then, the boys shook their sticks.

"Give us the money or else," ordered the boy in a striped shirt.

"I have no money."

One boy grabbed his leg to pull him down from the donkey. Using his stick, Essy hit the boy on the head, sending him to the ground.

They gathered around Essy with their sticks on his chest.

"You know Mikhail is my brother, and if you touch me, he will kill you."

"We are not afraid of him or anybody else," said the bigger boy, then hit Essy on the leg. They began searching for his money. Essy struggled. One of the boys looked under his shirt and took out the money bag.

At that, Essy punched the boy in the face.

The boy with a striped shirt hit Essy on the head with his stick.. Essy got up and got on his donkey.

"I will be back with my brother," Essy said.

Essy entered the yard and walked behind the donkey. After taking the donkey to the barn, he went into the house.

Essy entered the room, bloody-faced and head down from the shame.

The family was sitting on the floor, drinking tea as he entered the room. Mikhail, who was fifteen and muscular with a cut mark on his cheekbone, stared at Essy. He put his teacup down, stood up, and walked to his brother, taking his hand.

"Let's go," he said.

"No, Mikhail, wait." When their mother inquired, she turned to Essy and said, "Come here, my dear, let me look at you."

He went to his mother and knelt.

"Money is all you're worried about, Uncle?" Mikhail said, his voice laced with anger.

"Goodbye, Mother. I will take my horse." On his way out, he grabbed his stick from the corner of the room by the door.

A little later, they arrived at the boy's village riding a horse with Mikhail in the front and Essy in the back.

The boys sat on the steps of a house.

"It was them," Essy pointed to the boys.

Mikhail jumped off the horse, and then Essy jumped off. Mikhail holds his stick in one hand, and with the other, he holds Essy's hand. They got closer to the boys.

"Which one hit you on the head?" He asked Essy.

"It was the one wearing a striped shirt," Essy pointed to the boy.

"You stand here, brother."

Mikhail walked to the boys.

"I want all the money that you all took from my brother."

"What money?" The boy in the striped shirt said with a smirk on his face.

Suddenly, Mikhail struck the boy on the head with his stick. The other two got on their feet with sticks in their hands. In no time, Mikhail had the boy down and injured. Mikhail pushed the end of his stick against the boy with the striped shirt's neck.

"Give me all the money," Mikhail ordered the boy.

The boy removed the money bag from his neck and handed it to Mikhail. Mikhail gave the bag to Essy and asked him to count. Essy counted the money and nodded.

The door to the house opened, and an old man stepped out.

"What is going on here?" he asked.

"These boys took my brother's money and broke his head. We do not want more trouble, so go in and shut the door now," Mikhail told the man.

"Is that right, boys?" he asked.

One of the boys nodded yes.

"You boys get in right now. I am sorry about what happened. Who are you, boys?"

"We live in Shahrivar. Ghobad is my uncle, and I am Mikhail. This is my brother Essy."

"I apologize for what happened. I have heard about you." Tell your uncle Abas, the butcher, sends his regards," the old man told Mikhail.

"Okay, sir. Let's go, Essy." They got on the horse and rode away.

Chapter 3

Star-Crossed Lovers

Mikhail is now twenty, and a secret love attraction is built between Mikhail and Tamara (17). Mikhail is handsome, tall, kind, a tough fighter, a gambler, and a drinker.

The beautiful young Tamara had been Mikhail's neighbor since childhood, and they secretly met and talked. All the girls have their eyes on Mikkail and wish to marry him despite his bad reputation among the older village residents.

Esrafil, on the other hand, is a handsome, shy, and hard-working young man who is planning his future and hoping to marry Tamara someday. He was unaware of his brother's relationship with her. Her beauty and kindness were the talk of the village people.

"Would you take this butter to Tamara's family?" Rayhan asked her son Esrafil.

"Yes, mother," said excitedly.

"No. Essy, I will take it to them," Mikhail told his brother.   "You worked all day in the field."

Essy, disappointed, nods his head okay.

Mikhail stood at Tamara's house door, combed his hair, knocked on the door, and waited. Tamara opened the door.

They were excited to see each other.

"Hello, Tamara."

"Hello, Mikhail. I can't talk to you. My parents are home," she whispered.

"It's okay. Mother asked me to bring this butter for you." he handed the dish to her. As she reached for it, he held the dish and her hands.

"When can I see you? My whole family is going to a wedding tomorrow. Can you come to our house? You can bring the dish, then," Mikhail said.

"I am also going to the wedding with my parents."

"Try to sneak out for a few minutes. I will be waiting for you.

"I will try," She whispered.

"I will leave the door unlocked," he told her.

The following night, they met in the barn. The blanket was on the floor. The sunset light came in from the window and shone on them as they lay on the hay.

Mikhail was on top of her, and they kissed.

"I hope your parents agree to you marrying me," He whispered.

"I begged my mother to persuade my father. I hope he agrees. I love you so much. I swear if I can't marry you, I won't marry anyone else." They kissed more.

"I can't live without you being in my life. If you marry someone else, I will kill him," Mikhail whispered.

***

It is the annual harvest celebration day. All men wore hats, and women wore colorful clothing, hoping to catch a guy's attention. As Mikhail was stick-fighting with the village boys and winning all the fights without any scratches, the village girls clapped and gazed at him with admiration.

Tamara and Mikhail looked at each other and smiled. Essy saw.

A few days later, Mikhail asked Ghobad to talk to Tamara's parents so that they could get married. As is customary, the girl's parents invite the boy's family.

Mikhail and his family were at Tamara's house. Tamara's parents, Maryam, her older sister, and her brother, Abe, sat on the floor having dinner.

Finally, after some conversation, Ghobad proposes that Mikhail and Tamara get married with Tamara's parents' permission.

After the kind response from Tamara's father, he did not accept the proposal.

Her father replied, "With respect for you, Mr. Ghobad and Miss, Rayhan and Mikhail, unfortunately, he does not present himself as a proper suitor, with no job to support a family. Everyone in the village knows he is tough and handsome, but women need a home and a provider. We will wait to see if he changes his ways.

On the other hand, Mr. Esrafil is known in the community as a hardworking and kind young man, and I know many families would gladly marry their daughters to him. He owns a cow and some land, which is very important."

At that moment, Mikhail stormed out of the room, went home to the barn, and started drinking.

Later that same night, Mikhail, along with five men — three of whom were brothers and two others—sat on the floor, with a fabric spread out in front of them. Plates with food and bottles of hard alcohol were on the cloth. Two kerosene lamps on the floor lit the food and drink area. They were playing cards. All the men were wearing hats, as it is a custom in the village of Shahrivar.

The room was quiet and smoky from cigarette smoke, and the eyes were fixed on the hands and cards.

"No cheating, guys. This is going to be a fair and square game. Right?" Mikhail asked as he looked at the brothers and then turned to the watchdog.

"Keep your eyes in everyone's hands, especially on the brothers."

They continued playing as Mikhail closely observed the cheating brothers. After a few minutes, Mikhail put his cards down, finished his drink, placed his glass on the floor, and picked up his money.

I said, "No cheating. I am out."

"There was no cheating; you were losing, and that is why you are quitting. Put your money down and leave the room." The biggest brother of the three said to Mikhail.

"Guys, are the brothers cheating?" Mikhail asked.

The other two men nodded yes.

" Shut up, Mikhail. Put your money down and leave before you get hurt," one of the brothers said.

"Did you say shut up to me? I have had enough of you brothers."

Mikhail kicked the big brother in the face. Then, as the other two brothers got up, he hammered one of them in the face. The guy flew back, hit the wall, and lay on the floor. Then he took the third one down and pulled a knife on him.

"Next time, I will carve your fucking eyes out. Do you understand me?"

The guy nodded yes, and Mikhail left the room.

***

After several months, Tamara's father died in a horseback riding accident. Forty days after Tamara's father's death, Esrafil's mother asked Tamara's mother for her daughter's hand in marriage to Esrafil.

Mikhail was heartbroken and drank more.

***

It was fall and harvest time. Tamara was in the orchard picking pears. Mikhail was on his horse, riding through the area. He saw Tamara, rode into the orchard, dismounted his horse, and said hello. At first, she ignored him and looked away. Then, they hid behind the horse.

"I wanted to say goodbye. I am leaving in the morning to go to Russia. Turn and let me see your beautiful face once more

27

before I leave. You will have a good life with Essy. He is a kind and hardworking man. He will make a good father and a good husband."

Without looking, she asked, "Russia? But why are you going to Russia? There's such a mess there." She turned; her eyes filled with tears. "What about me? What about the love that you always spoke of?"

He walked close to her and took her hand.

Tamara whispered, "I know Essy is a good man, but I will die here with you so far away. Please, anywhere but Russia. Please, somewhere so I can see you occasionally. Many people have moved to Tehran, so why not go there?

"I want to go away; I want to go to Moscow, where I was born, and I want to die there and be buried next to my little brothers. I hope that I find their graves so I can get headstones for them." He choked. "They had been lonely for too long. There is no one there to go to their graveside. I will miss you, Essy, and especially my poor mother. I hate that evil Ghobad." Suddenly, she hugged him hard.

"So, is this goodbye?" She wept with her head resting on his shoulder. He touched her long, braided hair and then pushed her back.

"We do not want anyone to see us like this," he said, his voice thick with emotion. "I hope you know that I am not a bad person; I just have unhealthy habits. I know I will never make a good husband."

"It is not fair. Please write," she begged of him. Then she looked at him and kissed him. "I love you," she whispered. She placed his hand on her chest.

"This heart of mine will always beat for you."

He placed his hands on her face and whispered, "I love you, and I love my brother. I will not hurt him. I should go before someone sees us." He gets on his horse and rides away as her teary eyes watch him disappear. She leans her head against the pear tree and weeps heavily.

Chapter 4

The Sinners

Tamara and Essy got married, and soon they had their first child, a beautiful boy, whom they named Nader. Rayhan loved him dearly.

Rayhan was heartbroken by the loss of her two boys during their childhood, the loss of her dear husband and lover, Mami, and finally, Mikhail leaves her. She might have been able to hide her tears, but sometimes her red eyes would reveal so much.

Nader is now three years old. He is a handsome and strong boy who loves to help with chores around the house and the farm.

Tamara was very happy with her life, especially with her hard-working husband. It had been about three weeks since Esrafil went to the big city of Tehran to find a job, seek a better place to live, and achieve success in a city that would provide more opportunities for their children and a much better education.

Tamara was washing clothes in a tub, and Nader was Chasing the chickens in the yard.

The old wooden door opened to the yard, and Mikhail entered with two suitcases. Tamara looked at him. He was dressed in nice clothing. Her eyes filled up as their eyes met. Nader ran to his mother and looked at her.

"Don't you cry, mother? Are you scared of that man?" He picked up a rock and threw it at Mikhail.

"Get out of our house." he said.

Then he ran to his stick on the ground, picked it up, walked over to Mikhail, and shook it in the air. Michael smiled and then set down the luggage.

"Go away. I hit you." Nader yelled.

"I am your uncle Mikhail; didn't your papa tell you about me?
Nader looked at him. "Yes, he did."

Tamara was speechless, dried her eyes with the corner of her
dress, then covered her hair with the scarf draped over her
shoulder and rose to her feet.

"Honey, this is your uncle, Mikhail. He used to live here with
your father four years ago, but he went to Russia. Say hello to your
uncle."

Nader said hello.

Mikhail looked at Nader.

"What a handsome boy you are. Where is your father?
Working at the farm?"

"No. Father went to Tehran to make money."

"I see." Mikhail looked at Tamara.

"It is so quiet here. Where is everyone?" He asked.

"They went to Ardebil for business and to do some shopping.
They will stay there tonight."

"I see. Of course, he would not take you. Can I sleep in the
guest room tonight?" he asked.

"Yes, I'll go inside and make tea and something for you to eat.
You must be tired."

"Just a little bit. I would like to go to the barn to get cleaned
up."

"I will bring you some towels."

***

It was night, and they sat on the floor with a cloth spread out,
food, and a lantern in the center of the cloth.

They ate in silence; Tamara and Mikhail exchanged glances.
Nader eyed his uncle warily.

"The bed is made with clean sheets," she said shyly and
nervously.

"Would you like to see a picture of my wife and my children?"

31

"Yes," she said in a soft voice.

He pulled a wallet out of his jacket pocket, took out a photo, and passed it to her.

She looked at the picture and gave a deep sigh.

"Your wife is very pretty. Your children are beautiful."

He just stared at her.

"Do you love her?" She asked softly.

"No, there is someone else that I am in love with."

A few minutes passed in silence.

"I have a gift for everyone; I will give it to you in the morning."

"Nader, do you know what a train is?" Michail asked.

"No," he said.

"Your grandfather fixed them. He was a train engineer. Maybe you will be an engineer someday. You have seen cars, right?"

"Yes, in Ardebil."

"The train is like many cars connected together. When I give you the toy train, I will explain more."

"The food was great. Thank you." Mickail said.

"You're welcome. So, are you working?"

"Yes, I'm a tractor mechanic. I wish I were a train engineer like my father. But they pay me well. I like my job. Anyway, I'm going to get some rest. Do you know where Uncle keeps his medicine? I need a little to help me sleep."

"I will get you some after I put Nader to bed."

"Okay. Good night, Nader."

Nader regarded him as if he were a stranger.

Tamara took Nader to his bed, covered him with a sheet, and kissed him good night. Then, she picked up the lantern and walked out, shutting the door quietly.

She knocked on Mikhal's door.

"Yes," he said.

"It's me. I brought you some of Uncle's opium."

"Come in. I am in bed."

She shut the door and walked to him as he sat up.

"Thank you. Are you happy? he asked out of nowhere.

"I suppose I am. He is a very loving and caring man. However, I still think of you all the time. I miss you a lot, Mikhail."

"I miss you as well. But we can't talk like this."

"I see that you've been drinking," she said.

She walked to him and sat beside him. Took his hand and kissed it.

"This isn't right," he whispers.

"No. Just hold me in your arms for a moment."

He held her.

"Whenever I go to the barn, I think of you and the night we met there. I wish you had taken me with you."

"I wish that I could," he kissed her hair

She looked up and kissed him.

They make love.

She left the room feeling sinful.

He drank more and hit his head with the empty bottle. She went to her room, sat, and quietly wept.

Early in the morning, half asleep, she heard the door. She waited for a few minutes, then left the room. She softly knocked on the guest room door, but there was no answer. Her eyes filled with tears. She opened the door. There were several gift boxes on the floor by the bed, and a note on one of the boxes.

Please give these gifts to everyone. Tell Mother that I love and miss her very much. I will be back someday. Please let everyone know that I had to leave. There was a line that was scratched out. She crumbled the paper and wept.

How can I live with this shame? Oh, dear God, please forgive me.

She went to the barn and took a bath.

Tamara would struggle her entire life to forget her sin. Throughout her life, she could not comprehend how she could have committed such an offense and betrayed her husband. After the birth of her second son, Babak, she was uncertain whether Babak was Mikhail's or Esrafil's child. Mikhail never returned to Iran or contacted his brother Esrafil again. A few years later, Esrafil learned that his brother had died in a factory accident at work.

Mikhail had a girl and two boys. The younger boy's name was Esrafil, and the older boy was named after their father, Mami. His daughter was named Rayhan.

About a week later, Esrafil returns to his family.

Tamara was in her kitchen making bread in the oven, which was dug into the floor and lined with clay. She placed the circular dough on the round cushion made of hay in the center, which was covered with fabric. Then, she slapped the dough against the oven's wall, where dried cow manure served as the heat source. A chimney was positioned right above the stove to allow the smoke to escape from the room. Later, this chimney will reappear in the story.

Outside, in the yard, Nader was feeding the chickens.

Rayhan, Esrafil's mother, always felt she had no choice but to marry Ghobad. So, she was always unhappy, and for that reason, she ate more than she should have, resulting in some weight gain. She was a thin and beautiful young lady when Mami and she met on the train. She missed Mami terribly and missed her two boys. Her two boys were buried somewhere in a Moscow cemetery, far away from her. She wept in her lonely times. And now she is heartbroken because Mikhail lives too far from her.

Rayhan was busy making plate-sized patties from cow dung and slapping them onto the clay wall to dry in the sunlight. She sang and wept She was old, hopeless, and

34

heartbroken. Besides, Ghobad always talked about marrying a younger woman. The big lump tightened her throat.

This dried manure would serve as the heat source in winter and be used for cooking when wood is unavailable.

Chapter 5

His True Love

The old wooden door opened into the yard. The kind and pleasant Esrafil stepped into the yard, carrying a suitcase in each hand and wearing a brand-new cowboy hat.

Nader looked at his father and ran to him. He put his arms around his father. Essy put the luggage down, bent over, and kissed Nader.

Rayhan called Nader, "Come here, my dear, and pour some water so I can wash my hands." Nader ran to his grandmother, picked up the brass pitcher, and poured water over her hands. She washed them and dried them on her apron. Then she and Nader walked to Essy.

"Oh, my dear son, you're back! Come give me a big hug and hold me tight."

He wrapped his arms around her and held her.

"I missed all of you. Why are you crying, my dear mother?" Essy asked.

Rayhan spoke through tears. "Mikhail came and went. I didn't get to see my boy. Essy, I wanted to see him before I die. I think he's still mad at me for marrying your uncle. We were all in Ardebil. I'm going to die heartbroken, my son."

"Grandma! Momi and I were here, and we saw him. He brought a toy train from Russia for me. Don't cry, Grandma."

"What do you mean? He came and left? Please don't cry, Mother. You know how much Mikhail loves you; he would never do anything to hurt you. He must have a good reason. Please don't think that way about him, Mother. For being such a tough guy, he has a soft heart."

"Yes, he came a week ago, dropped off some gifts for everyone, and left that same night, she said through her pouring tears."

Ghobad steps out of the barn with a pitchfork and a dog beside him. The dog raced over to Esrafil and barked while wagging its tail.

"Is that hat for me, Essy?" Ghobad asked.

"Yes, uncle."

"Did you bring some money to buy cattle or sheep?"

Rayhan whispered to her son, "Say no."

"No, Uncle, I didn't work that much this time."

"You should have stayed longer," said Ghobad.

"No, Uncle, I plan to move to Tehran next year after we finish with the crops."

"Great, then you can send me more money to purchase some land," Ghobad said.

"We will see Uncle."

"Essy is probably tired; he should go in, eat something, and rest," Rayhan said.

"Where is Mother, Nader?" Essy asks.

"At home, she is making bread."

"Can you go and tell Mother that I'm back?"

"Yes, Father." He ran out of the yard.

Inside the house, Rayhan sits beside her son and whispers.

"Ghobad was very sick last week and made his will, leaving everything to his two sons, including your land and cattle. Do not trust him with anything. See what he did with your father's money, and how he made you and Mikhail quit school, even though he had promised your father he would not do that."

"I know, Mother, I always think about that. Maybe we should blame Uncle for the way Mikhail turned out."

At this time, Nader walked into the room with a box.

"Father, look! Uncle Mikhail brought me this train from Russia. He said I should become a train engineer like Grandpa Mami."

"Yes, honey, you should. We'll look at your train in a minute, okay?"

"Yes, Father. Mother, and I have missed you."

"You know what, Nader?" his grandma said.

"What, Grandma?"

"You are the apple of my eyes."

"I know, Grandma," he said and left the room.

"I need to get everything ready for supper. You should go to your wife and get cleaned up for supper."

Esrafil stood up and helped his mother to her feet.

He kisses her on the cheek three times. "I love you, mother," he said and left the room.

After a nice dinner with his family and his wife, he got up and walked, carrying a piece of luggage in each hand. Tamara held a lantern to light the way to their living quarters across the yard. They went up the steps and entered their living room through wooden double doors.

"I missed you terribly," he told her.

"You were away for too long, and I missed you a lot."

"Dear Nader, please change into your pajamas so you can get ready for bed."

"But, Mother, I want to see what Father has brought for me."

"Father is very tired; he needs to go to bed. However, early in the morning, we will open the luggage to see what Father has brought for us, and you can show your train and get it running so he can see."

"Okay, Mother." He walked over, kissed her, and then approached his father, hugging and kissing him. "Father, have you seen a real train?"

"Yes, in Tehran. They are very long. When we move to Tehran, we will all take a short trip on it."

"Okay, Father," he said, goodnight, and left the room.

"How was Tehran? Did you like it?" she asked softly.

"It's a nice city, and I liked it. I worked at a bakery, and it really wasn't too bad. It's a bit hot, but he paid well; the owner is Armenian. He has a spacious room upstairs where he lets the workers sleep."

"That is very nice of him. You can tell me more tomorrow. Let's go to bed now," she said seductively.

"We'll go to bed soon, but first, I've got something for you."

He reached into his pocket, pulled out a small box, and handed it to her. She opened it and took out a golden necklace. She removed her scarf and unbuttoned her blouse before putting the necklace around her neck. She turned, and he fastened it for her. Tears well up in her eyes as he turns her around to see her expression.

"What's the matter, my dear? Don't you like it?

"Nothing, I love it. Let's go to bed; he's probably asleep now." She took his hand, and they walked toward their bedroom.

"My sister visited while you were away, and she mentioned that they like Tehran."

"Yes, it is a beautiful city, and many of our relatives live in the same neighborhood."

"Your step-brother Ali keeps saying that he wants to move to Tehran to live with us. He is so lazy and disrespectful to me."

Chapter 6

Promised Land

Rayhan dies in late spring of that year, before her son Esrafil takes her to Tehran as he promised.

After 40 days of mourning, Ghobad marries a younger woman.

In the summer, Tamara and Esrafil welcomed their second son, whom they named Babak, after a famous Iranian hero. The crops were harvested at the end of summer. Esrafil, along with his two sons and Tamara, moved to the bustling city of Tehran to take advantage of the opportunities it could offer their family. Leaving their peaceful village of five hundred people for the vibrant and booming city of Tehran was a significant change, but they quickly adjusted to the new lifestyle.

No one can predict the future or the outcomes of our decisions. Life can sometimes be nothing but pain and sorrow for some unfortunate, good people. Peace is like a kind guest, but one that visits briefly.

Tehran, a beautiful and vibrant city, welcomes countless people from diverse towns.

***

From 1925 to 1941, Reza Shah laid the foundation for a modern Iranian state in the Middle East during his 16-year rule. He ordered the construction of roads and tunnels, initiated train services, and established free hospitals, universities, and modern offices. Most importantly, he expelled all foreign forces controlling the banks and oil companies. He raised awareness about human rights and advocated for women's freedom, voting rights, and the right to choose their clothing. He imposed limits on Muslim clerics regarding their enforcement of Islamic rules.

In 1941, Reza Shah was forced into exile by Western countries.

Throughout history, a powerful country has often controlled how smaller nations operate. Reza Shah's son, Mohammad Reza Shah, emerged as the new Iranian leader. Under his leadership, Iran made rapid technological advancements and emerged as one of the world's most powerful nations in many respects. For some baffling reason, we cannot ignore that oil was one of the main factors. For oil or whatever other nonsensical reason, the US, along with a few European countries, chose to depose Mohammad Reza Shah, just as they did his father. They replaced him with an arrogant, uneducated, radical Muslim named Ayatollah Khomeini. This decision would plunge the once peaceful Middle East into chaos and war for many decades to come. In just over four decades, nearly a million innocent people have died. The ironic thing is that the same countries that played a role in regime change in Iran ended up going to war to overthrow the very Islamic government they had installed.

Radical Muslims have executed countless influential, educated, and innocent people. The country has been ravaged and destroyed since. Not to mention the wars and crises in the Middle East, which have caused millions of innocent deaths and immense destruction. Meanwhile, Western countries have been benefiting from lower oil prices.

Chapter 7

Life in the Big City of Tehran

In 1951, our main character, Babak, was born, and shortly after, his family moved to Tehran.

Babak's life journey is sure to be an interesting one. It is heartbreaking at times, with war and love in the background.

"The lines on the palm of your hand read that you will have an interesting life with two or three wives. I see that you will travel across the sea, unhappy, and return to Iran, where chaos awaits, but you will find some happiness. With all these obstacles, you will have a long life. I will pray for you," An old medicine man told Babak when he was just a young, mischievous boy.

The Medicine Man himself led an interesting life. He is believed to be a descendant of the Great Prophet Zoroaster. "Think no evil, say no evil, do no evil." This verse is known worldwide, but many people are unfamiliar with this Prophet.

At one time, Zoroastrianism was the most widespread religion in the world, particularly in Persia, now known as Iran.

***

Two young boys, Babak, five years old, and Nader, eight years old, run up and down the marble steps of the old two-story house, laughing and giggling as they tag each other while racing up and down the stairs. The brothers' sweet laughter grew louder with each trip until the door to the first-floor apartment swung open as they reached the bottom step. It was their landlord, a tall, grumpy old man.

In a deep, angry voice, he asked, "Boys, wait a second. What are you kids doing?"

The brothers stood side by side, holding hands.

"Haven't I told you not to play here on the steps?" Without waiting for a response, he stepped closer, reached out, and slapped the youngest boy, Babak, across the face.

The poor boy flew back from the blow, hitting his head against the wall behind him. After regaining his balance, the five-year-old placed his hand on his face and looked at his older brother, trying not to cry. He rubbed his cheek to numb the sting. He glanced down and burst into tears as a wet spot spread down the legs of his khaki pants, forming a puddle at his feet. The older brother, Nader, walked over and held him, attempting to comfort him while glaring at the old man. It was all he could do to avoid insulting and swearing at their landlord.

"What are you looking at? Do you want me to slap you as well?" the old man asked, shaking his fist in the air.

The older boy squinted, his fingers clenching into trembling fists as he glared at the man with hatred.

"You had better send your mother down here to clean up that mess," the man commanded.

The boys stomped up the stairs. With his emotions raging, the older brother could contain them no longer and yelled down, "You stupid old man, I hate you."

When the brothers reached the top of the steps, Nader muttered, "I'll kick his butt when I get older and pay him back for this." He reached over to wipe the tears from his brother's face. The boys entered the apartment and headed to the kitchen, where their mother worked.

She glanced over and saw young Babak's teary eyes and flushed face.

"What has happened, my dear? Why are you crying?"

"That ugly, old man slapped him," Nader said, bursting into tears himself as he held his brother's hand. Babak began crying again at the thought of the incident.

"What was the reason for this? Tell me what happened," their mother asked. Closing the distance to her boys, she hugged and kissed them.

The boys told their mother of their innocence and how the landlord was so beastly and mean to them.

"Nobody can hit my brother, nobody," the eight-year-old said, breaking away from his mother's arms. He walked over to the wall, unsuccessfully holding back the tears. "I'm going to sell popsicles and funnel cake to make money and save it so we can buy our own home," he said, frustration and anger on his face.

"We'll buy ourselves a house soon. You and Babak will have your own bedroom." Tamara smiled softly at her boys. A tear rolled down her cheek as she understood her son's anger. She had been saving money and pinching pennies wherever she could. Many nights, she fed her family onion soup with bread to keep food expenses down, and often the family went to their cold beds with inadequate food in their stomachs. She calmed her boys and went down to take care of the mess at the man's doorway.

At dinner time, when her husband Esrafil "Essy," came home from the bakery where he worked, he passed a bread bag to Nader. Nader cut a piece of French bread and passed it to his brother, then cut a piece for himself. The family discussed the entire incident. Their father grew angry about the whole thing. "I will have to talk to the man."

"Yes, father, you go down and kick his butt and slap him hard too," Nader said with a chewing and vengeful tone.

"No, Essy," Tamara pleaded. "Please do not; I don't want a fight. He'll kick us out. Many landlords prefer not to rent to tenants with children, and they may refuse us. Let's just be patient, and we'll show him. Like my father always said, "A bad landlord could make you a homeowner.""

44

"Okay, okay," her husband said, looking at his family and nodding. Once he regained his calm, he continued, "Well, I have some good news. I've found some land near our relatives; we'll be able to build our house the way we want very soon, and you will have your cousins as playmates."

Several months later, the boy's father came home from work and announced it to the family as they sat on the floor eating dinner. They will be purchasing the land in the next couple of weeks. "So, what do you boys think?"

The boys cheered, and Nader said, "Father, I've saved some money I can give you for the land."

The boys had always been little entrepreneurs, selling things on the streets. They took advantage of the season and the hot summer days to sell funnel cakes and Popsicles. They pushed their wheeled cooler up and down the neighborhood and shouted to the other children. They saved every penny they could from their sales.

"No, son, you keep it for the house. I have enough to cover the cost of the land, but we will need more later. I hope to have the house ready before the new year, and we should be able to move in with some luck on our side."

Everyone raised their water glasses and smiled as they toasted.

Their father set his glass down and cleared his throat. "Your Uncle Ali is going to come and live with us soon, and he'll help complete the house."

"Oh no, not again," a frown replaced the cheer and happiness on Nader's face. "I like Uncle, but he's rough when he plays around. He is just so mean. Can't I help with the house, Father? Does he have to come?" You know I am strong, Father. I can pick up fifteen bricks at once," Babak chimed in. "I am strong, too, Father. I can pick up Nader."

"Yes, I know. But we need his help as well, Nader. We must complete the house as soon as possible, hopefully before the new year. Their father smiled as he looked over at his wife. "We also

45

have some news we have not yet told you. Soon you will have a new brother or sister."

"Is this true?" Nader asked as he looked at his mother. "Another brother?" he inquired.

"Only the lord knows the answer to that question, but don't you want a sister?"

"Yeah, I want more brothers to play with, too," Babak agreed. "Yes, but only after having five brothers."

She smiled at them. "Yes, son," their mother answered. "I will ask your uncle to be gentle when he comes. We need his help, though."

Nader nodded, looking down at his feet. "Okay, Mother, I understand."

Chapter 8

Grief in the Big City of Tehran

Ali, the boy's thirteen-year-old uncle, had lived with the family for several weeks. As usual, he teased and joked with the boys, often telling them stories from Shahnameh. He reenacted the characters and played music with his mouth.

Ali would rough them up as he had in the past when the children's parents weren't home. They tried to keep their distance as much as possible from their young prankster uncle.

The boys and Ali sat on the floor as he recited from Shahnameh.

"Ali, I need to go out to get some groceries. Please keep an eye on the boys and continue sharing your stories with them. Tamara turned to her two sons. "You boys behave now. I won't be very long." She leaned over, kissed them both, and then rubbed their heads before leaving the room. She hugged and kissed her two boys almost a hundred times a day.

"Don't forget to get some soda, Aunt Tamara. We're almost out." Ali called Tamara "aunt" due to their age gap, though she was his sister-in-law. Once she shut the door, he turned to Nader and Babak. "Okay, let's wrestle."

"No, Mom said no roughhousing. Tell us more stories," Nader replied.

Babak chimed in, "Mom doesn't want us to fight."

"Oh, come on, you chickens!"

"We are not chickens; we are not supposed to fight." Babak stomped his foot.

"I will be nice. I promise." He grabbed their shirts and lifted them off the floor.

Nader surrendered; he knew he couldn't stop his uncle, so he lunged for Ali's legs to bring him down. Ali, who had an unfair

47

advantage due to his height and age, wrapped his arms around Nader's neck and squeezed as hard as he could.

"Ouch! You are hurting me," Nader screamed.

Nader's younger brother walked over to them and tried to pull on Ali to get him to release his big brother. The uncle pushed back at the five-year-old as he held even tighter with his other hand around Nader's neck.

Nader released his uncle's leg and screamed, "Let me go, you jerk," then bit into his uncle's hand.

Ali raised his knee and struck Nader in the scrotum, then shoved him back against the wall and said, "No biting you, stupid brat."

Nader reached down, cupped himself, and doubled over. Nader's face paled as he curled up on the floor and wept. His little brother quickly ran to his side and reached out his hand to Nader's shoulder. "Are you all right, Nader?" he asked with great concern. "Are you okay?"

Nader tried to hide his pain and nodded yes.

"Oh, he is all right, he is just faking it," Ali was rubbing his hand where Nader bit him.

Nader lay on his side, cradling himself and rocking gently to alleviate the pain. He moaned softly.

Babak knew that his brother was hurt badly. As he placed his hand upon Nader's face, Babak turned to Ali and said, "You stupid idiot, you hurt him badly." Tears swelled in his eyes and ran down his cheeks.

"Sorry," Ali said halfheartedly as he left the room and headed to the kitchen to grab a cold soda from the cooler.

Nader lay still, taking slow, deep breaths.

"Here, drink this. It will help you," Ali insisted.

Nader shook his head and stayed lying on the floor.

"Come on; sit up and take a drink," Ali demanded again as he reached over his shoulder and tried to force Nader to sit up.

Nader complied with his uncle's request and sat against the wall, his legs straight out and his hands cupped between them.

Ali, realizing his nephew was not faking his pain, grew worried. "Come on, drink this." He watched as Nader took a small sip and stopped.

"Drink more," Ali insisted.

Babak stood intently watching the two older boys, hoping the situation would somehow improve. The door opened, and Babak jumped.

Tamara walked in and called out, "Boys, I'm back."

"Mom, come quick—Uncle Ali kicked Nader in the privates," Babak cried out as he ran and tugged at his mother's skirt. She dropped her groceries and rushed to her son's aid. When she entered, she found Nader crouching against the wall, holding himself, while his uncle stood nearby, looking guilty with a bottle of soda in his hand.

"What has happened, son? Oh my God, son, what happened?" she said as she saw the pale-looking Nader. She looked at Ali with insistent eyes. "Well?"

"Nothing, really; we were just playing around. I don't know what happened," said the boy's uncle.

Nader turned and glared at Ali, a pained expression on his face.

"Come on, honey, let's get you up and head into the kitchen. I bought you some figs," she said as she stood, unaware of her son's pain. She tried to help him to his feet. Nader let out a cry from the pain.

"Mom, I can't stand up; it hurts too much," he cried.

"Oh, all right, you stay, and I will bring them to you," she said as she walked over to her bags of groceries. She turned, gave Ali a disapproving look, and said sarcastically, "Well, thank you! Thank you, Ali."

Tamara returned to her son to give him the precious and rarely purchased fruit he often begged for. However, she noticed he had no interest in what she offered. Nader's condition was worsening.

Babak was deeply worried about his older brother, who was incredibly close and inseparable. Babak patted his brother on the arm and asked, "Do you want to play with the kite together later?"

Nader tried to be strong for his little brother's sake, responding by squeezing his hand and giving him a soft smile. "Sure, that would be nice," he whispered, kissing Babak on the forehead.

Ali had kicked Nader's main artery, causing him to bleed internally. He lost consciousness, and the family took him to the hospital. The trip was lengthy due to the distance and traffic. When the doctor delivered the shocking news, Tamara fainted and fell to the floor.

Chapter 9

The Mourning Chant

It was a gray and gloomy fall day, the season of death, when the color withers from the trees and the grasses dry. A large crowd gathered in the alley; all dressed in black. This would be their choice for the next forty days; however, for some mothers, it would last the rest of their lives. This custom showed respect and honor for a loved one who had passed away.

***

Four men walked in front, carrying the small wooden casket on their shoulders as the weeping crowd followed them, chanting a prayer to Allah. Babak's father walked, holding his son's hand while wiping the tears from his pale face with the other hand. Babak's tears streamed constantly down his young cheeks. As they proceeded, the mullah walked just a few steps ahead of the casket, chanting a melancholy song, which the crowd echoed in a soft, unified voice.

It was difficult for family, friends, neighbors, and shopkeepers who knew Nader not to cry. He was a polite, respectful, sweet, and caring boy who was dearly loved. Babak's aunt, Maryam, helped her sister maintain balance. Tamara's legs felt weak, and her body was numb from the shock and sorrow she was enduring. Her scarf, which usually covered her thick, dark hair, had slipped off her head, exposing for the first time in public what she had always been forbidden to show. The family hadn't eaten for two days. She was a beautiful, twenty-five-year-old, broken-hearted mother who took the loss of her young son extremely hard. She wept softly and sadly, singing a lullaby to her son as the tears kept flowing.

Finally, the close-knit group of friends and family made their way to the small neighborhood cemetery. A tiny hole had been dug to place the casket within. The four men carefully lowered the casket onto the ground beside the eternal home. As the crowd gathered, they touched the casket with trembling hands, saying their last "goodbyes" and tossing rose petals on the grave along with their prayers. Tamara and her only living son fell to the ground, crying. Tamara reached up and began pulling her hair out by the roots. Moe, Babak's cousin and best friend, sat down sadly next to Babak and placed his hand on him for comfort.

Ali, Essy's stepbrother, who caused Nader's death, stood at a distance under a tree, feeling remorseful and weeping.

"Please bury me with my dear child; I can't let him go by himself. Please, Lord, take me too. He needs me," Tamara cried out as she reached for a handful of dirt and poured it over her head. She grabbed another fistful of soil and poured it over Babak's. Family members tried to comfort the distraught mother and her son as the hired men stepped forward. They each held a corner of a white cloth to lower the casket into the hole. After the small wooden casket reached its final resting spot, the men began shoveling the dirt to cover it.

"No! No!" Babak cried out as he stood up. He ran to a large cedar tree, and his cousin Moe followed him. Babak put his head against the tree and hit it, weeping so hard that he lost his breath. Suddenly, his sadness burst forth in uncontrollable sobs. His little heart ached, shattered by the loss of his best friend and brother. Babak cried out, "I want to go with him."

"I know," Moe whispered, crying as he patted Babak on the shoulder.

Babak's father approached the two boys and pleaded, "It is time to go home now." He bent down and cradled his only son as he wept. His heart was filled with grief and pain for Nader.

"I am not going home again," Babak whispered, a lump in his throat. He banged his head against the tree.

"Okay, Moe, could you stay with him and bring him later?" asked Babak's father. Patting his son on the head in understanding of the pain, he turned and walked away, weeping.

"Yes, uncle, I will, don't worry," Moe replied, tears streaming down his face.

***

Several days and nights filled with grief, sadness, and fasting passed. One day, Tamara followed Babak as he entered the cemetery. He walked to Nader's new grave, lay on the ground, and wept profoundly. Tamara stood behind a large tree. She cried as she watched her son. After a few minutes, she approached Babak, lay by the grave, and wrapped her arm around him.

Filled with loneliness and loss, Babak would walk away from home searching for something he had lost. He always ended up at the cemetery, pouring a bowl of water he fetched from the nearby creek to wash the small headstone, then covering it with a handful of wildflowers. This became his routine day after day. He would wander through the neighborhood, sometimes venturing far from home, humming a particular melody to himself.

It was getting dark, and Babak had not yet made it home. Tamara went to the cemetery, but he wasn't there. Upset, she walked from one neighborhood to another in search of Babak, believing he should be home. After an exhausting search, she found her sister Maryam and Babak sitting on the floor at home, enjoying tea and cookies. She grabbed her son in her arms, weeping with relief.

My poor sister, we have been waiting for you to return home. Babak came to our house, and I was in disbelief, not knowing how he found us so far away. Anyway, he can't continue this. I know how close they were to each other, but I'm sorry you have to do what our mother did to our brother when he kept disappearing.

***

Babak sat on the floor, playing with his brother's train and listening to his mother and aunt talk. After his aunt left, his mother asked him to sit close to her. He sat next to the kerosene heater, which had a spoon heating on it.

Honey, we must discuss you leaving home and going so far away. You know that lately, children have been going missing in town. We have discussed this, and you promised not to do it again, but you repeatedly disappear for long periods. This needs to stop, and I need to do something about it before anything happens to you. "You know I love you, and this is why I have to do this," she said with a heavy heart.

"Do what, mother?" he asked, wearing an innocent expression.

Ignoring his question, she said, "I need to take your sock off."

"Okay, Mother, I can do it," he said. He removes his socks.

She looked at him and thought only of the terrible act she was about to commit against her son. She grabbed a potholder and removed the spoon from the heater; she hesitated for a second, then took his foot and raised it, pressing the hot spoon onto the bottom of his small foot.

He clenches his teeth, struggling to hold back his tears.

She placed the spoon on the floor and took him in her arms. With a lump in her throat and tears in her eyes, she said to Babak, "Don't you know that your father and I miss Nader just as much as you do? Sometimes I hear your father crying in the middle of the night. We both miss him terribly, honey. So, please do not do this again. Any time you want to go to the cemetery, tell me so we can go together and take some water and flowers."

"Okay, Mother. I am sorry."

54

Chapter 10

The Kite Keepers of Heaven

Babak is seven now, flying his kite, his excitement reflected in the grin on his face. He is proud of how high he has flown this precious kite in the sky. Nader and Babak made this kite, and it was the first time since his brother's death that it had been flown, its diamond shape swaying from side to side. As the wind picked up, he released more line for his kite to ascend higher and higher. The boy ran backward, and it appeared smaller and smaller. Suddenly, the end of the line slipped from his hand. Babak ran with all his might, trying to catch the string to regain control. He ran faster and faster, reaching out and almost touching the string. The string teased and enticed him. He put all the energy he had into trying to catch it. He had to catch the string.

Before he knew it, Babak looked down and saw that his feet had mysteriously left the ground. His momentary panic was squashed by his determination to catch the string, so he continued with the realization that he was flying. The height was thrilling and enjoyable, but soon, the kite disappeared into the clouds. With it, his smile vanished. He could not let the kite get away—not this kite; it was the kite he and his brother, Nader, had made together. This kite was precious. Babak reached up into the clouds and continued searching. He heard a voice call out his name.

"Babak, look this way to your right."

Babak looked at where the voice came from and saw the kite's line dangling. Without hesitation, he began to follow it again. Through the clouds, Babak saw haziness and fog; he could barely make out a boy flying his kite. He looked around, astonished; the clouds were now full of kites. They were all sorts and sizes – a dragon, a butterfly – so many, and all so different. Babak thought to himself, these must be all the lost kites. As he looked closer, he saw that each kite was held by someone: boys, girls, young people, and old people. The whole sight amazed him. He felt the soft, puffy clouds as they tickled his bare feet.

"Babak, come a little closer," said a familiar voice.

He tried to get closer to the indistinct image of the boy flying his kite.

"Nader, is that you?" Babak called out.

Yes," the voice replied. Babak started running to get closer to his brother.

"No, no, please stop right there, Babak. You cannot come here. I will hold on to your kite until it is time for you to come and be with me."

"No, Nader, I want to come and see you and be with you. I miss you so much. Mother and Father miss you too. I have a new baby brother; his name is David. I tell him about you and all our fun times together. He is tough just as you always were," Babak said as he tried to get closer to his older brother. "Oh yes, we have moved to our new house, and I wish you were there; we all miss you." "There is not a night that I do not think of you and tell you good night before I go to sleep."

"Yes, I know my dear brother," Nader responded.

"Nader, but how did you get there?" Babak's eyes filled with tears. "I thought you died. I saw them put you in a coffin and bury you, how?"

"It's magical; everyone ends up here," Nader said. "Babak, listen. You cannot come here now; it is not time for you yet," the voice called out. "Mother, Father, and David need you. You need to protect David and teach him to be smart and strong. I will be watching you from here every day. Kiss everyone for me and give them my love." The voice began to fade away.

"But I want to be with you, don't go," Babak called out. He closed his eyes, and tears began streaming down his face.

Opening his eyes, he found himself lying in bed with his mother sitting beside him.

She had heard him crying and had come to comfort him. She could not keep the tears from streaming down her face. She felt sorrow and missed her eldest son as well.

"You seem to have had a dream about Nader, honey." She rubbed Babak's back and brushed her hand across his forehead. Then, she started to comb her fingers through his black hair.

"Nader said I could not go with him," Babak cried. "He said to kiss you and Papa and send you his love. He was happy to hear about David and wished he could be with us."

"Oh, I wish too," said his mother, wiping her eyes. She leaned over, kissed her son on the head, and hugged him tenderly. A lump rose in her throat, and she began singing a sad song that always seemed to echo through the small rooms when her thoughts lingered on her eldest son. As she held Babak, she rocked him and murmured the words softly.

"You know what, mother?" Babak asked.

"What, honey?" She replied.

"When I die…"

His mother interrupted him. "Please do not say that," she said as she teared up again.

"Okay, Mother, when I see God, I will tell him I do not like him. If he were a good God, he could have saved our Nader.

Chapter 11
Trapped in the Chimney

Babak's ancestors migrated and settled in the village of
Shahrivar in northern Iran, right at the foot of the Alborz
Mountains, where the Silk Road was established centuries ago.
Babak and his family returned to their village each summer to
visit their grandparents and assist with the farm chores.

Babak, David, and their cousin Moe headed home,
laughing and having fun as usual. They decided to use their
slingshot skills again. They pushed a stick into the soil and
packed it with dirt to ensure it stayed in place. They jabbed
pears onto the top of the stick. Each boy shot rocks at the
pear, watching it shrink as pieces broke off with every hit.

As the boys took turns, they noticed two birds coming
and going, carrying bits of worms to their nest. Moe aimed his
slingshot at one of the birds.

"No, no, don't shoot at them. We don't want to kill
them. I want to go up there and get one of their babies,"
Babak said. Moe stopped in his tracks and obeyed his cousin.

The three boys from the city went to the barn and
returned with an old wooden ladder. They set it carefully
against the barn and attempted to level the ground to prevent
it from wobbling. The ladder was finally secured, and Babak
volunteered to climb it before Moe could.

"Aunt Tamara, look Babak is climbing the ladder to get
the birds," his cousin yelled.

The swallows had made their nest in a crack beneath the
roof's soffit. Babak reached toward the nest to take one of the
babies when suddenly, their angry mother returned.

She flew at his face, screeching and scolding him for
trying to go near her little ones.

Babak was startled by her sudden return, lost his grip on the ladder, and fell backward, landing in a pile of dirt.

The other boys hurried to his side to check if he was injured. He was covered with dirt and seething with anger.

"Dammit! It is just not my day," Babak said as he pounded his hand on the ground. His mother was outside, hanging clothes on the line to dry, and when she heard the commotion, she ran to her son's side to see if he was injured. Babak lay back and stared up at the sky.

"Oh my God – son, what happened? Are you okay?" she asked with deep concern.

"He was trying to get one of the baby birds from the nest, and the mother bird swarmed at him, and he fell," David answered in a guilty voice.

Their mother gently leaned over Babak, brushing off the dust with a concerned expression. "You know she was only protecting her babies. If it were me, I would have done the same. Honey, you must be careful and stop doing these crazy things," she said, softly kissing him on the head. "Now, you boys go on and get cleaned up. Dinner will be ready soon!"

"Ah, can't we play a little longer? We'll play safe," pleaded their cousin.

"Okay, just be careful. I will call when your supper's ready," she said, giving in to her nephew as she brushed her hand through his thick, wavy hair.

Babak's sister, Mehri, overheard the conversation while sitting on the swing and asked, "Can I play too?"

"No, not this time," their cousin replied. "Besides, you are a girl; this is a boy's game." He walked over to the wall and said, "I will close my eyes and count to fifty."

"You go that way and I will go this way," Babak whispered into David's ear. Babak ran toward the tall birch tree next to the wall. He positioned his feet between the wall and the tree, working his way up to the top of the wall. He took off running until he reached the end, where the wall met the roof. Babak climbed onto the roof and yelled at his cousin,

"Okay, you can come and look for us."

He continued running on the roof and reached the middle. He spotted a chimney hole, typically used to vent smoke from the oven. These ovens were standard; nearly every house had at least one. They were usually dug into the floor, built from straw and clay, like all the homes made with the same materials. The ovens were about three feet deep and twenty-five inches in diameter, with enough openings to accommodate dough about sixteen inches in diameter, which was slapped against the hot wall for baking. The primary heat source for these ovens was cow manure. People would go outside to gather it, shape it into patties, and slap them onto the clay wall to dry. Once dried, they would pile it into a six-foot-tall cone and store it in the barn until needed, using it as a heat source on frigid winter days and nights.

Due to its location, winters in northern Iran often bring extremely cold temperatures to the region. The people in this village were resourceful and courageous, relying on many ancient home remedies and herbs for survival.

So, Babak decided this would be a good hiding spot and climbed in, lowering himself deeper into the chimney. He thought he could easily jump into the room, run through the house, go out the door, and touch the wall while his cousin was looking for him. But he forgot that the oven was eight feet directly below him.

Unfortunately, the chimney opening was narrower than Babak had anticipated. He couldn't squeeze through, even with his arms raised above his head. His shoulders were too broad, and he got stuck. The more he struggled, the worse it became. He called for help, hoping someone would come to his rescue.

The family in the house heard and went to the room where his feet dangled.

Ali tried to pull him down while the kids on the roof attempted to pull him up. Meanwhile, the straw and clay chimney scratched and cut Babak's sides and arms.

Finally, Ali stopped pulling Babak's legs. One of the stronger neighborhood kids pulled him back up and out of the chimney. Babak's family members came to help and were upset by the entire incident involving Babak.

"My son, you were very lucky that you did not fall into the oven with blazing fire. His mother yelled at him as he looked at her, embarrassed."

Step-grandfather Ghobad arrived and watched as Babak climbed down from the same tree he had used to reach the roof. Babak got on the ground and stood by the tree, shamefully.

His grandfather wore a big smile with his arms folded.

"Boy," he chuckled, "you have been so lucky today. They have told me about your encounters today. You must have the angels weary from looking after you. You know they have other children to look after and can't spend the whole day watching just you."

"I believe my angel is looking out for me, and it's my blessed brother Nader, Grandpa," he said softly.

"I know," said his mother. "Tomorrow, I will invite the old medicine man and have him pray for you, Babak. I have told you, he can work miracles; he is a descendant of the prophet Zoroaster, and they say he can tell your future."

"Yours should be interesting, Babak!" Moe said.

Babak asked his mother, "Does the medicine man know about people's future?"

Tamara told her son, "Yes, honey, he can be right sometimes. When your father and I got married, we went to him for a blessing. He told us then that our first child would die at an early age, and unfortunately, he was right." Tamara leaned down, hugged him, and whispered, "Our future is written on our foreheads, and we cannot change it, so don't worry about it. Don't worry, you will see him tomorrow, and he will pray for you."

"Shall we go eat now? We have had enough entertainment for tonight," said Grandpa.

The following day, the medicine man visited the grandfather's house. Babak and his mother met him. Feeling somewhat fearful and ashamed, Babak gazed up at the tall, bald, strong man with large hands carrying an intricately carved walking staff. He wore a peculiar old hat, quite different from what everyone else in the village wore. Around his neck hung a necklace inscribed "Say no evil, do no evil, and speak no evil," shaped like a winged king.

Babak's mother told the man about all the mishaps Babak had experienced the previous day. His mother continued, "And the last thing he did before supper was to get stuck in the chimney. He had everyone worried," she declared.

The children and family members had all gathered to see the old medicine man and his wondrous methods.

David, giggling, said, "It was funny!" Babak turned to him and shook his head.

Babak approached his mother. "Momi, I want to ask you something."

"What, honey?" she asked.

"I want to tell you in your ear," he told her.

Tamara knelt.

"Is he going to punish me with his stick?" he whispered.

62

"No, honey. He is going to pray for you. Go to him and don't be afraid."

Babak approached the intimidating old man.

"I will pray for this lad. I will pray loud for his health and safety," he said as he placed his large hands on Babak's shoulders.

"Thank you, kind sir," Babak's mother said as she bowed respectfully.

With his right hand, the man grabbed Babak by the collar and lifted him as high as possible towards the almighty. The old man began shouting from deep within his throat as he looked up into the sky. No one understood what he was saying; it was like he spoke a different language. It was a special Zoroastrian prayer passed down to him from his elders and their elders, who had lived there for thousands of years.

The village of Shahrivar is situated near Mount Alborz, and it is said that the Great Prophet Zoroaster is buried in this area.

The medicine man's prayer continued as everyone stood and watched. Finally, his prayer ended, and he carefully lowered Babak to the ground. Babak's body was limp, and he looked pale. He was more frightened of this man than of being caught in the chimney. The medicine man knelt to Babak's level and examined Babak's hands, studying them intently, then suddenly spat on Babak's forehead. He began to rub it into Babak's skin with his palm. Holding onto the back of Babak's head with his left hand, he palmed the spit more forcefully with his other hand, as though trying to ingrain it into his very skull.

The family members all stood around, puzzled by the sight. Sweat dripped down the man's forehead as he finished his prayer.

"Now, son, you must still be careful— but God will watch over you. You will have a long and exciting life and will die a natural death. You will have children to carry your family name on, and you will have two or three wives."

63

At this, Babak raised his eyebrows, smiled, and gave the children watching thumbs up.

Chapter 12

Death in the School Dungeon

His heart trembled as he sat in the dungeon, in the damp, dark, cool air enveloping him. This was a twenty-foot human-made underground cave, once used for storing water, and now serves as a place to punish misbehaved students.

Babak's feet were swollen and sore from being beaten by the school principal's order due to Babak and his cousins' mischievous and dirty game that they played on other students in the schoolyard.

The cold brick floor provided some relief from the pain. Sparks flickered in the darkness, accompanied by the click, click, click of a cigarette lighter. Then, a loud fart erupted in the silence, followed by a bright flame.

Hearing laughter from about five feet away, Babak recognized it as Moe. Moments later, the lighter's flame illuminated his cousin's face. Moe was still squatting with the lighter held between his legs.

"I swear to God that you are retarded. God! How could you play such a dirty prank on my friend and hurt him like that?" asked Babak. "What you did was very mean, Moe. He could have been killed. It was supposed to be a game! You turned it into a bloody one; this is the reason we are down here."

"But he didn't die, did he?"

Asad stood up and painfully stepped over to his cousin Moe, slapping him on the back of his head. "You dumb shit!"

"It's not over yet. I'm worried one of these days you'll hurt someone and end up in jail," said Babak.

"I wonder what jail is like," Moe teased.

65

"I don't know, but he did not do anything to you, did he? All I know is that I will not play any more of your dirty games or get involved in your fights. I want to put more time into studying."

Flashback

During recess, the boys were everywhere in the middle school playground. They always tried to show off their skills and enjoyed gaining the attention of the other kids by playing one of their favorite games choskhorak, which means smelling a fart. In this game, one must be able to perform somersaults and flips.

One of the boys bent down, his hands resting on his knees, while his friend mirrored his position. Another young boy knelt on his hands and knees, positioned between the other two with his head close to their butts. He hollered out, "Come on."

Asad, one of the three cousins, went first. He placed his hand on the back of the brave boy on the ground and flipped over the other two boys using him as a springboard. Babak was next, followed by Moe's turn.

Moe came running with full force and placed his hand on the boy's back, bringing his head down to the boy's back as hard as he could before flipping over.

"Ouch! Goddammit!" the boy grunted as he stood up, rubbing his sore back. His eyes flashed with anger as he glared at Moe.

His teammates gathered around and asked if he was okay. They were prepared to stand up for him and confront Moe together.

Babak walked over to him and asked, "Are you okay? Sorry, Moe can be really stupid sometimes."

"I'll be okay." The boy's voice was quiet yet filled with anger.
"Do you want to quit the game now?"

I have to pay that jerk back.

"Are you sure?" Moe asked.

"Come on, I'll be on the ground this time," Babak said, trying to smooth things with the two boys.

"You butt kisser!" Moe said to Babak.

"He's my friend, and you know that!"

"Oh, he is your painting buddy." Moe said, his tone dripping with sarcasm.

Babak and Asad bent back-to-back, both hands on their knees and their butts touching. Moe took his position by kneeling on the ground, with his hands and knees on the floor, his back sticking out between Babak and Asad's legs.

"You better not fart, you jerk!" he said to his cousins. Then he told the other team in a high-pitched voice, "Okay, girls!"

The injured boy from the other team ran full force toward them and jumped, preparing to slam his head down onto Moe's back, but Moe quickly dashed forward. The kid hit his head on the concrete in the schoolyard. He rolled on the ground, grunting in pain. Blood flowed from his head and face.

Babak removed his shirt and said, "Here, put this on your forehead to stop the blood."

Moe walked over and kicked the ground, muttering like he always did afterward, "Oh crap! Oh crap!"

The bell rang, signaling that recess was over. The principal yelled from his second-story window, "Children, make your way to the classroom now!"

One by one, the boys crept away from the scene. Three custodians and a few teachers approached to investigate the commotion.

Moe, the main instigator of the entire episode, changed his chant to, "Shit, shit."

Babak knelt on the ground and helped the injured boy by dabbing the blood from his head and attempting to clean it from his face.

One of the boys shouted, "Oh God. Wow! Look at all that blood."

An older student, who was also well-built and larger than average, approached the scene. "Who did this?" he asked.

A boy from the other team spat, "It was Moe."

The older student turned to Moe. "Did you do this, Moe?"

Fearlessly, Moe shot him with a dirty look. "Yes, I did, and that's none of your business."

The principal made his way down from his office to the scene, tightly clutching a spanking paddle in his hand. He stormed over to the boys with raised eyebrows and his jaw clenched in anger.

"I want the students involved to come to my office, but everyone else needs to get to their classes immediately." He looked directly into Moe's eyes. "I want one of you to tell me what exactly went on here." Someone should take the injured student to the nurse's office.

In the principal's office, Babak, Moe, and Asad were asked to stand in the corner of the room. One of the three custodians stood ready with a cherry stick in his hand, while the other held a broom. One of the teachers had two pieces of rope.

"Asad, you are first. You know what to do," demanded the angry principal.

"Yes, Sir." Asad knelt, shaking slightly, and removed his shoes and socks. He got down onto the floor, lay on his back, and lifted his feet and hands into the air. The custodians immediately entered their designated area and understood their role in this punishment procedure. They tied both of

Asad's ankles to the broom and then proceeded to secure his wrists so he wouldn't pull them away when the punishment began. Asad glared at Moe with anger. Two big guys held each end of the broom, the man with the cherry stick stepped forward, and began striking the bottom of Asad's feet. Throughout the ordeal, Asad shot a furious glance at his cousin and troublemaker, Moe. Grinding his teeth, Asad restrained himself from yelling out in pain.

The man with the cherry stick moved from Asad's feet to his hands and yelled, "Open your hands if you don't want your fingers hit." After several strikes, Asad turned his head toward the wall, closed his eyes, and tried to hold back the tears of pain and shame.

"Enough! Get up and go over there. Stand in the corner and do not move." The principal's hard eyes conveyed his meaning.

"Babak, it's your turn," he barked, but when he turned around, he saw that Babak was already in position, ready to be strapped down and beaten. They followed the same procedure, but no one had to remind him to keep his hands flat to avoid getting his fingers struck.

The principal noticed and inquired about the blisters on Babak's hands that he had previously had.

"I forgot to do my homework, sir."

"Go ahead, proceed," said the principal with frustration.

Moe prepared for his turn by removing his shoes and socks, holding his head high. He walked over and lay on the floor to be strapped in. They proceeded with the same type of punishment, striking him forcefully while Babak and Asad watched. Moe showed no pain on his face, not even flinching; it seemed as if the blows did not bother his calloused hands and feet, almost as if he were enjoying it.

Moe's indifference further enraged the principal, and he roared out the order, "Take them down to the dungeon."

69

"Babak and Asad, I need to tell you something." Moe's voice sounded different in the darkness.

"What now?" Asad asked,

"Well, first off, I'm sorry about today. Sorry, I got you into trouble," said Moe. "I'm going to quit school."

"Yeah, right you are, sorry? Ha! I am sorry also to be your cousin!" replied Asad.

"I'm going to drop out of school. I create issues and constantly get you into trouble."

"You can't quit now. You need to finish the sixth grade at least so you can get a job," Babak said, worried.

Asad just laughed. "It will take five years for him to finish the sixth grade, Babak."

"He's right, Babak. We have all been held back in fourth grade twice because of me. " Moe said.

"But what are you going to do?" Babak asked.

"My father wants me to work for my brother in his auto repair shop..."

Babak nodded in the dark, considering this. "I think you could be an excellent mechanic."

"Yeah, I'll have my own Mercedes by the time I'm sixteen. Then we can go chasing hot girls."

The idea still didn't sit well with Babak.

"Can't you wait until you finish the sixth grade? I will help you study, but you must stay out of trouble."

"No, I'm done. I won't come to school tomorrow." The dungeon fell silent for a few minutes as the boys processed this news.

"Well, Moe, whatever, but I believe we should learn our lesson and focus on graduating and staying out of trouble from now on."

"I think it's a good idea, you work for your brother; he will keep an eye on you, teach you the trade, and keep you out of trouble," Babak said.

Asad mumbled, "I hope we don't die here like that kid did last month. But it might be better than going home and facing our parents."

Chapter 13

Attraction at the Museum

Since Babak and his cousins were disciplined in school, over three decades have passed. Babak's life has been nothing short of exciting, and he is expected to have two or three wives, as the medicine man told him and his family when he was just a young boy. However, the excitement and surprises for Babak do not end here.

After more than two decades, Babak returned to Tehran, Iran. In his late forties, Babak is handsome, with a touch of gray hair, and is well-dressed. His three-year-younger brother, David, is muscular with short hair, and he drives while Babak sits in the passenger seat. Babak looks out the window. The pollution is thick, the city is crowded, all the women are fully covered in hijabs, and the men are entirely covered in pants and long sleeves. He was trying to catch up with his old neighborhood and all the changes that had taken place in Tehran since he moved to the United States. Babak shakes his head as they pass through vaguely familiar areas crowded with an uncountable number of people on the streets, along with bumper-to-bumper cars and motorcyclists. Almost all the street names have changed.

"It is going to be extremely hard to overthrow this brutal and corrupt government; they have the Revolutionary Guard and foreign mercenaries working for them, in addition to their Mozdours and Besieges (highly paid bullies that walk among the people in civilian clothing). They are free to do as they please. All these groups are drug dealers, human traffickers, rapists, and torturers," David said with anger in his voice.

"A peaceful movement is not the solution at all; this government is an evil and heartless organized mafia and a cartel. They have tortured so many people and killed so many innocent people to satisfy their greed under their damn Islamic religion. It was the same bastards who stabbed me when I was going to college in America," Babak said.

"These mafia mullahs certainly have taken complete command and have raped our country in the name of the Islamic religion. At the same time, they send their spoiled rotten kids to America with a load of money to splurge on their whim," Babak said.

David watched the traffic while driving and added Babak's words. "The last time you were here was about ten years ago. Now, look at what they've done to the country. They keep everything under their control, and they've created such fear that no one dares to speak up, but soon, a bloody revolution will unfold."

"Yes, a bloody one. And all these bastards will be hanged. A day of revenge to live for," Babak said.

Babak recalled the 1970s in the same neighborhood when:

There is light traffic, and women stroll through the town in Western fashion: short miniskirts that expose their skin and hair. Most couples hold hands, and few men wear shorts. We see many in jeans and many in suits as well. Some women wear hijabs.

"The people are afraid to stand up against this government for their God-given human rights due to the fear of being arrested, imprisoned, tortured, or raped. We know what happens in those prisons; the bastards rape innocent teens and virgins. The religious leaders claim that this way, the demonstrators would go to hell rather than to heaven." David explained.

"Are we going to find a parking spot near the museum?" Babak asked as he looked at the busy city street.

"Yes. We will have to walk a couple of blocks to the museum," replied David. "Do you see, Babak, what these goddamned people have done to our city and country? They have

destroyed the beautiful parks and the mountainsides. They
sell, develop, or do whatever they please with anything they
can get their hands on. The prices of everything have
skyrocketed, and the number of drug users and prostitutes is
sickening. It is that crooked government family of 1000
causing it all."

"So much has happened, and I was not informed at all.
Are the guys still active as opposed to the government?"
Babak asked.

"Yes, the ones who are still alive and not imprisoned,"
David responded.   "Oh, here we go," he said, nodding
toward a parking spot. They park the car and walk toward the
museum.

As they entered the museum's exhibition hall, they were
greeted by the beautiful sounds of classical music.

Babak looked around. "Thanks to Farah and Shah, they
made significant contributions to Iran's arts and culture. Farah
was a strong supporter of contemporary art and collected
many famous pieces. She purchased works by Picasso,
Matisse, Van Gogh, and many others to be exhibited in her
newly founded museum. I saw many of them. "I wonder what
happened to all of Farah's collection and all the Persian
treasures," Babak asked.

"They are all in the hands of the mullahs and their
gangster partners, and by now have probably been smuggled
out of the country and sold to Arabs in Dubai," David replied.

Babak glanced at his brother and nodded.

The brothers walked into a portrait exhibit hall, and
Babak stopped to study a painting of a shepherd boy. "This is
a nice painting. I wonder who the artist is?" asked Babak.

"I am not sure, but I have seen his work in the
newspaper recently," David said. "I, too, can't read his name."

"I can't read his name either," Babak agreed.

"Oh, excuse me, sir; he is an art teacher at the university. His name is Ali Rezaee," replied a beautifully dressed woman wearing a scarf, who stood behind them. The woman was young and attractive; she had a friend with her who was equally striking, with a band-aid on her nose and dressed nicely.

"I love his work," she added.

"I like his work too," her beautiful friend commented.

"Are you an artist too?" Babak asked.

"Yes, we both study art at university, and we both enjoy abstract art.

"Are you guys artists too?" the girl with a band-aid on her nose asked.

"I dabble in art a little bit," Babak said.

"This painting is nice," David said, pulling Babak's hand to the piece he was referring to, taking him away from the two girls.

Babak didn't want to leave his conversation with the two girls.

"Yes, it is," Babak replied. Turned back toward the young girls and said, "Perhaps we will meet again?"

"Maybe, perhaps," replied the girls in unison.

An elegant, slender woman in fashionable black clothing, her head covered with a scarf and in her thirties, the "Rule Enforcer," stood by the doorway. She gave the brothers a disapproving look and shook her head.

A little later, David and Babak chatted with the same two young girls. Then, the rule enforcer approached them.

The rule enforcer whispers to Babak in a bitter tone. "Excuse me, sir, you are not allowed to speak to strangers here."

"We are not strangers, Ma'am; we have already met," Babak whispered.

"You should not speak to them unless you are related, sir. I'm sure you understand this simple rule."

" I don't understand it at all, along with the many other rules enforced in this country," Babak whispered.

"Well, you know, sir. Sometimes, speaking your mind can get you in trouble in this country. I would be more careful if I were you."

"You are right, ma'am,' Babak agreed.

David interrupts, saying, "Sorry, ma'am, we understand. Good-bye."

The girls smile and wave goodbye.

"You are married," David hissed to Babak.

"They were so beautiful," Babak said.

"You should see a doctor, Babak. I am sure that you have been a sexaholic for a long time."

"You are right, David, but what will the doctor say? Don't have sex," Bab

"I don't know, but those girls were likely gold diggers. They seem only interested in you to get into the United States. Once they get there, they'll leave you and your foolish self."

"Your wife is a very nice lady; it's best not to hurt her.

"She was a nice lady, but it's over between us. Sarah and the kids will be happier if I'm not around them. She said that."

"I don't understand. She seemed so nice on your last visit here, and everyone loved her. The two of you looked so happy together. What went wrong? All I know is that you two were crazy about each other and looked great together," David said.

"Sarah and I didn't share a bed for almost six months, and I remained loyal to her. It took a lot of willpower to turn down the beautiful ladies who visited the gallery or took painting classes, not to mention the gorgeous models who showed interest in me."

"Fate, David, fate. Maybe I should have listened to our parents and married Layla," Babak said.

"Maybe, but who can predict these things? Marriage is such a complicated relationship. I heard from one of her cousins that Layla got married to a fanatic Muslim guy who made her life miserable. They have two children; after a long struggle, she ended up divorcing him. Last I heard, she was living in Florida," David said.

"That's unfortunate," Babak sympathizes.

"You are right, Sarah was a very nice person, but in the last few years we have had many problems," explained Babak. "That is why I want to move back to Iran. I plan to stay and not even look back again. Maybe I could go up North of Iran, find a small town, and live there peacefully," Babak confessed,

"There is no way I can live here in Tehran."

"What about your kids and your properties?" David asked.

Silence for a minute.

"They are not kids anymore. They wouldn't care what I do or if I ever go back. But she? That's a different story. We have some properties we can sell for a decent price. I'm thinking about buying a home here in Iran. I want to drive up north to explore the area and see what the property costs are like. I guess I'll worry about that later," Babak whispered.

"Here comes that rule enforcer woman. Let's get out of here," David advised with a look of caution. "There's a great coffee shop very close to the museum; we should go there and talk. You'll love their creampuffs, and they have good coffee too," David said.

The brothers sat silently in the busy coffee shop, gazing out for a few minutes as the noise of people talking and laughing filled the room. They were deep in thought.

Babak placed his coffee cup back on the table and broke the silence. "We used to call that street the Lover's Lane," he sighed. "I have so many great memories from the seventies there."

"First, I'll tell you about Layla. After I completed all the paperwork for her and brought her to America, we spent a lot of time together. After being with Roya, I realized that Layla wasn't for me; she wasn't good in bed at all. I'll tell you about Rafeegheh and Roya later," but first, let me finish by telling you about Layla and Sarah."

Chapter 14

The Love of Layla for Babak

It was the 1970s, and Babak lived in the United States. He was going to college there to study architecture; that was his plan and intention anyway. He had high hopes and big dreams.

It is night as we enter the kitchen of a moderately clean apartment, and the light is on. On a small kitchen table are books, paper, pens, pencils, dirty dishes, an empty wine bottle, and two empty wine glasses. We leave the kitchen and enter the bedroom.

A lamp lights the room on the nightstand. Babak is in his twenties, handsome and athletic. Layla is also a beautiful, dark-haired woman in her twenties, and they are making love. Babak is on top, his hand in her hair. They are both nude under the sheet.

"Please don't mess up my hair, Babak. I had it done earlier today, and I want to show it to my friends later when I return to my dorm," Layla whispers.

He removes his hand from her hair and continues to make love to her.

"Have you talked to your mother at all today?" Layla asked.

"No," He growled.

"My mother spoke with your mother, and they discussed the details of our engagement and briefly talked about our wedding."

"Yeah," He grunted.

She kissed him on the lips.

"Oh, my mother reminded me again to be careful; she said to have fun but to try to stay a virgin until our wedding night."

"Oh God, oh God," He cried out.

I don't know how to tell her that I'm taking pills and that I'm no longer a virgin. Oh dear, are you coming?

"Yes," he said, out of breath.

She stayed quiet for a minute. He rolled off her and lay on his back next to her. He thought about the times with Roya and their hot, passionate lovemaking. He remembered Rafeegheh's sweet kisses and touches and how much he wanted to make love to her in the way she desired. He recalls how much she wanted him to make love to her. Even today, he treasures the photograph of both and what she wrote on the back: "You can have me any time you wish." Layla distracted his thoughts.

"Oh yes, my parents have invited your parents over for dinner. They want to get together before your parents go back to Iran," she whispered.

"That is going to be an interesting night," he murmured.

"Promise not to say anything that might upset my parents."

"I will try my hardest."

***

Layla, her parents, Babak, and his parents were sitting at the table enjoying a colorful Iranian meal in Layla's parents' apartment.

Akbar, Layla's father has a short, stubby beard like many radical Muslims, while Kobra, her mother, wears a scarf. Esrafil, Babak's father, has dark, neatly combed hair and a clean-shaven face except for his mustache. Tamara, Babak's mother, is beautiful and also wears a scarf.

Akbar wipes his lips with a paper napkin and starts by saying, "Well, Mr. Esrafil my friend, and Mrs. Tamara, we hope that with God's help, you have a safe trip back to Iran. We need to be patient. Ayatollah is trying to make Iran a good Islamic country."

"You mean free water and electricity? What a big lie and a deceiving promise that was. I was hoping you wouldn't bring this up again. After all the damage they have done to the country. I don't understand why you still support these evils. We grew up together, and we have been like two good brothers. Don't forget that we both became wealthy during the rule of the blessed Shah. We attended the mosque almost every Friday and donated generously. But the mullahs brainwashed us. They fed us a lot of nonsense and propaganda. Now that the truth is out about Islam in Iran and their corrupt government, you still choose to live in your denial and praise these evils." Esrafil said with a soft, yet bitter voice.

"My dear friend, I do not live in a world of denial. You are losing faith in Islam," Akbar said.

"I am not losing my faith; I have entirely given up my religion, like many other intelligent people in Iran."

"Don't say that, Mr. Esrafil," Kobra says.

"My dear friend, let's go back 1400 years. The people you believe in attacked our great country, killed the men, raped, and took our girls and women as slaves, burned, and destroyed everything, including libraries, Zoroastrian religious temples, and centers, and forced them to leave Iran or accept Islam, or be killed. And now this government has done nothing but that, killing and raping our children. What is going to make you wake up, Akbar?" Esrafil asked.

"We don't want to talk about that. Perhaps these people should avoid making the un-Godly accusations about the government, and they should refrain from spilling into the streets to demonstrate. They know what will happen to them," Kobra said.

"Don't you think people are sick and tired of the rules that strip away their rights?" Babak told Kobra that you and your husband are just as guilty as those who perpetrate such evils.

"Mr. Babak, I have always thought you were an intelligent young man, but like father, like son," Akbar told Babak.

"Why do you rent an apartment here and spend half a year in America and the other half in Iran?" Babak asked Akbar.

The two families looked bitterly at each other.

"Hoping that after you and Layla finish college, God willing, things will improve in Iran, and we will go back home, never to return to this evil and Godless country again," Akbar said with a tone of hatred toward America.

"You do not appreciate what our God-blessed Shah did for Iran. You really should love America, which backstabbed the Shah and Iranians and put your evil leader Khomeini in power in Iran, so that Americans could get cheaper oil," Babak responded.

"Let me ask you something, Kobra. Would you have allowed Layla to marry an older man at the age of nine? And would you permit Mr. Akbar to marry maybe five more women besides you? Just like the laws in Islam say," Tamara questions.

"Of course not," Kobra answered.

"Then you are not a genuine Muslim."

Chapter 15

The Sweet Love of Babak and Sarah

A table in the college student center was set with pamphlets and flyers. On the easel was a painting of Ayatollah Khomeini, depicting him as a vampire with blood running down from his mouth to his beard. Babak talks to his friend Mike, an American student.

"America and Western countries have been engineering this revolution for Iran for a long time. First, they made the Shah seem like a vicious dictator by having the Ayatollah's followers kill numerous innocent people and place the blame on him. This Islamic group set fire to a movie theater, burning over six hundred people, including many children; the victims were locked in and could not escape. One family lost six children in this fire. This, too, was blamed on the Shah. At this time, people lost their faith in the Shah and began to hate him. My family and I loved the Shah but lost faith in him, but we immediately regretted our decision."

Two American students shout at Babak. "Go back to your own God damned country, you terrorist's son of the bitches."

Mike told Babak not to worry about the idiot. Most people here are angry with Iranians because of the American hostages in Iran.

Three bearded Iranians, who were not students, stopped and looked.

The stocky non-student points at the painting on the easel, which depicts the Ayatollah as a vampire.

"Who painted that?" he asked.

"I painted it; do you have a problem with that?" Babak asked. "You painted that? You're a dead man," the non-student told Babak.

Then, the same three guys knocked all the materials off the table and the painting onto the floor.

"Go to hell, you son of the bitches." Babak told the guys.

"We will send you to hell very soon, assholes," the tall and skinny guy said.

One of Babak's friends told Baba it was okay.

"We will take care of them later." However, his friend added that they could not do it in college, as they would lose their privileges to have a setup there.

The guys left. Mike walked close to Babak.

Mike whispered to Babak, "I have a pistol. I will bring it to your apartment tonight. I do not trust those guys; they might try to hurt you. If they come to your door and want to hurt you, shoot them, and drag them into your apartment, then call the police."

"Thanks, Mike. I'll be home after nine."
***

It was dark, and Babak and his two friends were on their way home on a dark street. Suddenly, the same three non-student Iranians come out of the darkness and attack Babak and his friends from behind, stabbing them in their backs with butcher knives. Babak saw his friends fall on the concrete sidewalk. He dropped his books, placed one hand on his back over his injury, and ran after the guys. As he ran, he left a trail of blood behind him. The stabbers disappear in the darkness. Babak sat on the sidewalk against the wall, bleeding.
***

Babak lay unconscious on the hospital bed, an oxygen mask covering his face and several IV tubes connected to the backs of his hands. His parents waited as the nurse, Sarah, a slender woman with blond hair and blue eyes, monitored the machines and recorded notes in Babak's chart. Tamara wept.

84

Two days later, Babak's parents, Layla, and her parents stood in the room. Tamara stood crying and distraught.

Nurse Sarah entered the room with a syringe in her hand.

"Good morning! If anyone needs coffee, water, or juice, there's a waiting room just down the hall to the left. Please help yourselves," Sarah kindly offered.

They shook their heads no.

"Okay, just let us know if you need anything."

Sarah walked to Tamara and hugged her.

Sarah told Tamara that he would be fine. Although he was hurt badly, he is doing very well now. He is a strong young man.

"Thank you, dear. God bless you." Tamara said.

"You are welcome," Sara said as she walked to Babak.

"Hun, I came to collect some blood samples. Are you feeling alright?" Sarah asked.

Babak nodded, then opened his eyes.

"A little pinch, okay? Your parents and family are here. Do you want to say hello to them?" Babak looked at her and nodded.

He looked at his mother, weeping, and nodded. He looked at his father and nodded. He saw Layla's parents. He quickly turned his gaze to Layla and nodded.

"You are doing well, Babak. I or another nurse will return soon," she said, holding two vials.

"By the way, Babak, your friends are also doing well. They will be fine."

He nodded, staring at her.

"May my wife and I see his friends later?" Esrafil asked Nurse Sarah.

"Yes, sir, you may."

Sarah walked to the door, and Babak looked after her.

Esrafil whispers angrily at Akbar, "See, Akbar, what kind of evils your people are. Even here, in America, Iranians are not safe.

You know, as well as I do, that if it had been a face-to-face fight, he would have torn them apart."

"If Babak and his friends hadn't handed out those papers, this wouldn't have happened," Kobra said.

"I can't believe how arrogant you are, Kobra," Tamara whispers to Kobra.

"Would you please talk about our differences somewhere else? This is neither the time nor the place to discuss these matters," Layla suggests.

"You are right, Layla," Esrafil agreed.

"Well, Esrafil and Mrs Tamara, we need to go get some clothes for Layla and then head back to our apartment," Akbar said.

"Bye," Esrafil said in a cold tone.

Babak gazed thoughtfully at the ceiling.

"Mother, father, you go. I will join you in a minute," Layla told her parents.

Her parents left the room. Layla held Babak's hand.

"I am so glad you are doing well; please do not take my parents seriously," Layla asked.

Babak looked at her and nodded.

"Someday, they will wake up, and everything will be fine. I have to go now. I love you, Babak, and I love you, Mr. Esrafil and Mrs. Tamara," Layla said and left the room.

"What an arrogant people; I do not understand them anymore. Anyway, Babak, Sarah is such a caring nurse. Isn't she?" Tamara asked.

Babak nodded and adjusted his mask.

"I like her," he whispered.

***

Sarah walked into the nurse's station holding two vials of blood.

"I heard that you like him, Sarah. He is so handsome," said Nurse Amanda.

"Like who?" Sarah asked.

"Your patient, Babak, don't play all dumb and naïve now."

"You can have him; I'm not ready for a relationship yet." Besides, he's going to be engaged to his girlfriend, who's a beautiful lady. His mother told me that the two of them grew up together," Sarah explains.

Finally, the IV and oxygen mask were removed from Babak. Nurse Sarah listened to his heart with a stethoscope. He caught a whiff of her perfume and closed his eyes.

"What's going on? Suddenly, your heartbeat increased. Relax, Babak."

"My father wants me to marry Layla because her family is old friends of my parents," he said nervously. Then he continued.

"We have been playmates since childhood. However, my mother says to marry the girl that you really love."

"Well, you will be released tomorrow. You need to stay home for at least one week and avoid lifting anything heavy. Make sure to take your medications, as we don't want you to get an infection and end up back in here again. Do you have any questions?"

He was nervous, and his voice was shaky.

"I want to tell you that you are a fantastic nurse, and the other nurses are great as well. I appreciate everything you did for me and how you saved my life. Yes, I do have just one question. I'd like to know if you would please have coffee with me sometime." Sarah turned and walked to the wall where the stethoscope belonged, placed it there, and then looked at him.

She shook her head. "I must decline. I'm sorry. But I believe nurse Amanda would like to go out with you."

"That's good to hear. I won't be doing everything you asked me to do, so that I can get an infection and end up here again. I'm serious. Just coffee, please? If you happen to like me."

"I need to attend to my other patients." She left the room. He watched her leave.

Sarah shook her head as she walked into the nurse's station.

"What?" one of the nurses asked.

"Well, he asked me out,' Sarah said.

"What did you say?" the nurse asked.

"I said no with a firm tone. But he replied that if I didn't have coffee with him, he would avoid taking his meds and try to get an infection so he could end up back in the hospital to see me again. Sarah shook her head.

"Wow, what a romantic boy," Amanda said softly.

"I told him you would go out with him."

"Of course, I would. He is so impressively handsome," Amanda said.

"Do you really think?" Sarah asked, her expression reflecting doubt, or something else.

"I certainly do; he seems like he comes from a good family. You are beautiful, and I know many guys would love to go out with you. You have been very determined not to get involved with anyone after what your ex did to you. Have coffee with him, as he suggested, if you're interested in him."

Sarah couldn't stop thinking about him. She wanted to make sure she liked him. After six days of waiting, she finally stood next to the phone in her living room, picked up the receiver, and dialed his number. He had been near his phone all this time, staying home as Sarah had asked him not to go to school. When his phone rang, he felt a sense of nervousness as he answered it. They talked and made plans for a date together.

Babak sat at a table in a café, nervously glancing at the door every time it opened and closed. When Sarah stepped into the café, she noticed him sitting at a table with a small bouquet. He was dressed handsomely. They sat in this quaint café, savoring coffee and sweets. A strange tension filled the air; he was captivated by her. She looked breathtakingly beautiful in her lovely dress and subtle makeup, eager to learn more about him. They talked and laughed together. Sarah admired him with her gaze before looking down at the floor. He watched her, not wanting to interrupt her thoughts or the silence.

"I need to go now, Babak," she said.

"Of course! Thank you for coming; I enjoyed your company. Don't forget your flower, Sarah."

"Oh, is this for me?"

"Yes."

She stood up and offered her hand; he took it in his.

"Have you been taking your medication regularly?"

"Yes, I was hoping to see you here, not in the E.R."

"Good decision. However, you need to be cautious. You look great."

"You look so different; I mean, good now and good in your uniform."

"Well, I'd better go. I'll call you sometime to plan our next date," she said.

"I will wait for your call and take my medication."

They released their hands, and she walked toward the door. He watched her walk away from him. She turned and waved goodbye, holding the flowers in her hand.

He sat there, staring at the floor.

It was night, and soft classical music played on the radio. Babak was studying at the dining table when his phone rang from the wall behind him. He turned toward the phone and picked up the receiver.

"Hello," Babak said, hoping it was Sarah.

Layla stood and leaned against the wall in her apartment, holding her phone.

"Hello Babak, how are you?" She asked, her heart pounding against her chest.

"Hi Layla, I'm doing well. How are you?" He felt guilty, cruel, and nervous all at once.

Layla asked with a shaky and innocent voice, "Why aren't you calling me? I've called three times. Where have you been? I thought you would be home at those hours. Are you doing okay?"

"Yes, I am fine."

"Are you upset with my parents, and is that why you are avoiding me?" She asked, irritated.

"Yes."

"I'm sorry about my parents, but we love each other and are supposed to get engaged soon. We can't let our parents and their differences get in our way," she said.

Babak, unlike his character, knew he was going to hurt her. He thought about his horrible decision, and still, there was a sense of violation in the air. He started speaking with a shaky voice.

"Layla, this is a significant issue, and in the future, it will become an even larger problem. I've given this a lot of thought. I'm afraid that you and I won't work in marriage, but we can still remain friends, as we have since childhood."

Layla's dark hazel eyes brimmed with tears.

"Friends?" she asked. "This is not you talking, Babak. I know you well, and I suspect you're hiding something. I want you to tell the truth: are you seeing her? I saw how you were looking at her at the hospital."

After a moment of silence, he simply said, "Yes, we met a couple of times. And I am sorry, but you and I are not good in bed."

Silence.

"Not good in bed? I see. Are you sleeping with her? That is how you are comparing her to me."

"No, we have had coffee a few times," Babak told the truth.

"Do you like her?" she asked, posing the tricky question.

"Yes," Babak answered truthfully.

"I am sorry that I am not as experienced in sex as some of the Americans or perhaps the Iranian girls that you have been with, like your beautiful classmate Rafeegheh," she said.

"Rafeegheh and I never slept together."

Layla continued with teary eyes and an angry, raspy voice.

"You are probably lying. Are you thinking about marrying an American after what they did to our country? How can you justify the deaths of thousands of people that they have caused?" Layla wiped her tears with her finger. She choked.

"I suppose I misjudged your character. After all these years together, how could you do this to me?"

"First, I have always liked you; you are a nice person. However, Sarah had nothing to do with what the government did. How do you justify your parents' actions, considering they are still supporting the killing of innocent people in Iran by the evil Mullahs?"

After a moment of silence and tears, Layla said, "I will always love you, and I wish you much happiness. Please tell me how I can forget about our sweet childhood memories. You hurt me, Babak, you hurt me so bad. No warning. No warning at all."

She hung up the phone and started bawling.

Babak sat at the table, feeling remorseful. "I had no idea how much she loved me," he whispered to himself.

Chapter 16

Love, Lust, Hurt

The shower door is steamed up; Sarah and Babak are kissing and touching passionately. They make love. She climaxes. Babak looks at her and smiles. They dry off. While keeping their robes on. Babak lifts her in his strong arms and carries her to bed. They make love again. He ensures that she has a completely enjoyable time.

Sarah and Babak are lying on the bed, with Sarah on top. She places her face against his chest, panting and kissing his neck as she whispers, "You were great, Babak. Wow."

Babak whispers, "You too."

He kisses her golden hair and runs his fingers through her hair. Thinking of Layla.

"Is it okay to run my fingers through your hair and make a mess?" he asked.

Sarah grunts with her face against his chest. "Yes, dear, you can put your fingers anywhere you wish and make a mess."

Sarah looked at him and smiled.

"I like you, Sarah," he said.

"I am very fond of you, too, Babak, but we hardly know each other," she said in a sweet voice.

"You know a little about me. Tell me what I should know about you. Or maybe it's better if you don't."

She rolled onto her back, looking at the ceiling, and they held hands.

Sarah mentioned she had told her parents that she had met a nice guy. I said I liked him and that he was from Iran. "By the way, my grandfather worked for an oil company in Iran, and he truly loved the Iranians and their country. These days, my father keeps up with the news about Iran; he says he doesn't understand those radical Muslims and how cruel they can be. So, my parents advised me to consider our relationship carefully."

"I agree with your parents and their concern for their daughter. Yes, radical Muslims are evil people. But did you tell your parents how my family feels about that religion?" Babak inquired,

"Yes, my father said that the men there mistreat their wives," Sarah added.

"That's not entirely true. However, I can assure you that I will never disrespect you or your family. If I do, it could be the end of our relationship, God forbid. Please inform them of this and ask if they would be willing to meet with me."

They held hands.

"Yes, I will, and I'm sure they would like you. But I need to tell you something else," she added.

"Is there more?" he asked, humorously.

Sarah spoke hesitantly. "I have a four-year-old daughter."

The room was quiet as she stared at the ceiling. His grip loosened around her hand.

"A daughter?" he asked.

"Yes, I will understand, respect, and accept your decision about our relationship. I know I should have mentioned it earlier, but I genuinely wanted to get to know you better. I thought that if things didn't work out between us, we could simply go our own ways. But I like you very much and I don't want to lose you."

After a minute of silence, "I have a four-year-old daughter echoes in his head."

"I can't do this," he thought.

Babak lay on his side, staring at a painting on the wall.

Sarah looked at him.

"You are avoiding looking at me, Babak. Do you want me to leave?" she asked.

He did not answer and kept his eyes on the same painting. Then he rolls on his back.

Sarah choked up. "I can't leave, not like this. Before I go, I'd like to ask for a favor. Could you please meet my daughter, Sophia? I have told her about you, and she wants to meet you. Will you, please?"

He lay there without saying a word.

Sarah continued softly during his silence.

"We were engaged and had plans and dreams of marriage and raising a family together. My fiancé and I decided to have a child early on in our relationship. Then I found out that he was fooling around with my younger, sleazy sister, the sister I had done so much for. When I confronted them, they moved out of state together without any shame or apology. I have disowned both because of that."

"We can go to a nice restaurant with Sophia, and I will pay for it," she said in his silence.

Babak looked at her.

"You ought to remind your parents about your ex-American fiancé, who shared the same culture as your family, and how it ended."

"I will, I promise."

"Life is a circus!" Babak whispered.

"Please give our relationship a chance," Sarah begged.

Babak shook his head. "I did, Sarah. I broke up with my fiancé. I broke her heart, her innocent heart. She loved me dearly."

Sarah turned and kissed him. "Please, Babak," she begged again.

***

Babak stood on the sidewalk beside a restaurant and watched as Sarah got out of her car and helped her daughter out as well. Sarah looked stunning and classy. Sophia was such

94

a doll. They approached him, and his heart trembled at the sight of Sarah.

"Hello, Babak. How are you?" she asked as she approached him.

"Hello, Sarah, I'm doing well, thank you."

"This is my daughter, Sophia, and this is Mr. Babak."

"Hello, Sophia! How are you?"

"I'm fine. Thanks."

"Aren't you a doll?" Babak asked with a grin.

"Yes, I know, Mr. Babak, nice to meet you too."

"I am starving, Sophia. How about you?" he asked with a smile.

"Me too, I can eat a whole cow," Sophia said.

Babak smiled as he looked at her.

"Let's go inside and order a few cows," Babak said with a grin.

Sophia gazed at her mother with wide-open eyes.

Sarah smiled. She was pleased with how he spoke to her daughter.

At the dinner table, Sophia was very polite. They talked and laughed while eating. Sophia kept glancing at Babak. She got up, walked to her mother, and whispered something. Then she returned to her chair, sat down, and smiled at Babak.

Sarah stared at the table, in deep thought, wondering what was next.

She placed her hand on Babak's and kissed him. "Thank you, Babak," she told him. He nodded.

They hugged and said goodbye outside the restaurant, leaving Babak and Sarah feeling uncertain. She needs to confront the pain if it is coming to her.

***

Babak went to his parents for advice. They sat at the table, ate pizza, and drank beer.

95

"Mother and father, I need to talk to you about Sarah. I told you that we have been seeing each other; we really like each other, and we want to get engaged. I met her family, and it seems like they like me. Her father is a doctor, and her mother is an author. They have an incredibly beautiful home. One thing I haven't told you yet is that she has a 4-year-old daughter; she is a doll. With that said, I need your opinion. Sarah told me that her parents liked me and they to her that Babak was a smart and handsome man."

"Honey, you are. However, I must admit that it usually doesn't work. We know Sarah is kind and beautiful, but having a child might be a problem later. Usually, the mother favors her child over the other children, especially if her child is a girl. I would say yes if she did not have a child, but the final decision is yours, my dear. I speak from my experience, but times have changed." Tamara told him.

She turned and looked at her husband.

"Am I right, Essy?" she asked.

Esrafil swallowed his food.

"Your mother is right. As your mother said, the decision is yours, my son. If you believe you love her, we trust your judgment."

***

Sarah had all the qualifications Babak desired in a partner. Moreover, he loved children. Babak felt satisfied and happy in every way imaginable. They spent a lot of time together, mostly in bed making passionate love, or camping and enjoying each other's company. Babak, Sarah, and Sophia enjoyed traveling together.

Babak was born and raised in a country with a unique way of life, characterized by its customs, traditions, culture, and strong family ties. He never thought that one day he would marry a woman who was not only unmarried but also had a child. Although he was raised in an open-minded family, his plans were not accepted by his parents and did not align with his own beliefs and standards.

***

Cultural dissolutions—this is what happened to Babak. In his case, it only took a few years for it to occur. But as he gets older, deep inside, he will struggle with the clash of two cultures and traditions.

After spending a few months together, they talked and planned their union. Despite his busy schedule with studies and a part-time job, the plan was finalized. Sarah dearly loved Babak and felt lucky that he was so good to her daughter; he was a better father than most men she knew.

Finally, the big day arrived. It was the late 1970s. Family and friends gathered at church, all of whom were Sarah's relatives. Although Babak's parents could not attend the wedding, they sent their love and heartfelt prayers from Iran.

Sophia served as a ring bearer and flower girl.

"Such a perfect couple," people told them so many times. They were both unusually handsome together.

"I now pronounce you husband and wife; you may now kiss the bride," the Preacher said.

Sarah and Babak kissed at the altar, and they looked at each other admiringly. Is this the true and everlasting love that some people speak of? It sure looked like one. She threw her flower bouquet in the air behind her.

***

Sarah looked so beautiful being pregnant with their first child. Sarah and Babak were fortunate and thrilled to find out they were expecting a baby boy soon after their marriage. Finally, the day arrived, and Babak drove her to the same hospital where he had met Sarah. Because Sarah was anemic, the doctors had to induce labor. Right after their son was born, Sarah and Babak were informed that the baby had swallowed some fluid; therefore, they took him to intensive care. It was a hard and stressful twelve days for the family, as Babak and Sarah spent day and night in the intensive care unit beside their son. They held the baby's hand and kissed his bruised little feet. His tiny feet were jabbed because of blood draws so many times.

After twelve days, their son was released from the hospital. He grew up to be a handsome and healthy boy. We can't forget about Sophia; she grew up as a beautiful and intelligent young lady, but her behavior reversed from good to bad when she turned thirteen.

    ***

Babak and Sarah, along with their twelve-year-old daughter, Sophia, and six-year-old son, Arash, were at the beach in their swimsuits. They looked beautiful as the family walked in the water, splashing each other while laughing and giggling. Babak stood behind Sarah, his arms around her, and kissed her when she turned.

"I love you so much, Babak. I feel so blessed. You fulfill my life, and I am truly lucky to have such a beautiful family," she told him.

"You and our children make me incredibly happy. I would be completely lost without any of you." The two of them hugged and kissed.

"Sophia and Arash go and play in the sand, finish your castle," Sarah said to the children.

The kids went to the sand and got busy building their sandcastle.

"Are you ready?" she asked, her voice filled with lust.

"Here in public?" he asked.

She took his hand and walked into the water almost to her neck. She submerged and pulled his swimming trunks down, then surfaced, smiled, and went down to pull her trunks down, and they made love.

***

Twenty years flew by quickly. Babak and Sarah's relationship gradually became colder and began to deteriorate.

An older Babak sits at the table with a plate of unfinished food before him. His arms are folded, and sadness and gloom are evident on his face as he stares at the floor. Babak's American wife, Sarah, is thin and attractive with blue eyes and blonde hair, sits across from him. She looks agitated as she gazes at him.

"Marriage is a partnership. In this partnership, when friendship, trust, and honesty deteriorate, so do lust, love, and care. The partners start to hate one another, and they can't see eye to eye."

***

"Babak, maybe you should just leave. You and the kids no longer get along. You are at each other's throats all the time. I am tired of being the referee," she said in a tone that Babak is now familiar with, reflecting the behavior she has exhibited towards him frequently over the past few years.

"What kind of referee are you? You always side with them, making me look like the bad guy, and that's our biggest problem," he said in a calm, soft voice.

"There's no point in discussing this matter any further, so it's probably best for the family if you move out. You can't expect them to adhere to your old-fashioned beliefs; this is America, not Iran. You make my daughter feel bad about dating and having a boyfriend. You give our son a hard time every time you see him because of his piercings and tattoos." Sarah rudely said to him.

Babak stared at the floor with his arms crossed.

Sarah continued, "This is what all the kids are doing these days. You need to adapt to our way of doing things. I don't want to choose between you and my children, but you give me no alternative."

"How can you say this to me after I have been a loyal and loving husband and father to our children? They aren't kids anymore. They don't care about you the way I do. They are just being lazy and want to live off us, like many other kids. And please don't bring my culture up anytime we have arguments. Look at your mother and her fooling around with other men. Your father is a nice man. After all, my parents were right about us getting married."

"About what? What do you mean?" she asked with a funny expression on her face.

"It doesn't matter now." Babak turned away and resumed looking at the floor. Sarah shook her head and placed her hands on her forehead.

"You are too old-fashioned. It was you who caused our daughter to disappear for months without any word." Sarah said, not looking at him.

"Right, Babak? Admit it," she uttered.

"Having dignity and pride and wanting them to attend college is too old-fashioned? Yes, I admit that. I always loved them, had good intentions, and wanted them to have a good future. I am sorry if that was wrong of me.

"Don't be absurd," she said.

"Didn't we have a wonderful time when our kids were little in Italy? We worked hard together towards our dreams, and now you're choosing them over me. Well, I won't ask if you're seeing someone. Why do you suddenly work overtime or go out with your co-workers?" he asked.

"When I am home, it seems like we fight all the time. I go out with friends to have some fun," she told him.

"I never do that," he said.

"Okay, I'll leave if that's what you want. It doesn't matter anymore, and I don't care. Remember, you are not entirely innocent yourself; you gave them too much freedom to do as they pleased. In fact, you paid for their tattoos. Where do they get money for their weed?" He asked.

"Whatever," she whispered and shook her head.

"For the sake of the good days we shared, I wish you all a happy life. But you didn't have to make our goodbye so ugly and bitter, Sarah. Please, after we handle our divorce and the settlement, do not contact me again."

A union that began with so much love and passion has now come to an end after about twenty years.

Chapter 17

Babak's Fate in Iran

The brothers still sit on the bench outside the coffee shop.

"When I reflect on my past relationships, I've concluded that love is all bullshit. From now on, I plan to have fun and enjoy being with beautiful women. Here, in front of you, I promise not to fall in love again." Babak promises his brother David.

"We'll see," his brother said.

"I'm sorry, sometimes things don't work out the way we wish, Babak. What are your plans now?"

"We have agreed to sell the properties and divide the profits between us. Everything has been paid off. I will have enough money to invest in a business and buy a home somewhere in Iran."

"That's good. At least the two of you are civil about divorce." David said.

Babak and David sat on the bench in the shade in front of the museum, on the sidewalk of a busy street. Both of them were deep in thought, ignoring the crowd, noise, and heavy pollution, which occasionally made Babak cough.

"We called this street Love Lane in the early seventies. I have so many wonderful memories here. Just look around and see the changes. I miss the good old days when the Shah was in power, and I am sure many people do," Babak spoke.

Chapter 18

The Love Lane

Babak drifted into the past as they sat on the bench—the same street, but with older buildings. Everything screams the seventies: the people, their clothing, and the cars. Babak (late teens), handsome, clean-cut, and well-dressed, walked hand in hand with his beautiful classmate and girlfriend, Rafeegheh (late teens), a uniquely beautiful, short-haired, stunning brunette. She wears a knee-high skirt and a low V-neck, sleeveless blouse.

***

Babak and Rafeegheh enter a crowded café and take a seat next to each other in a window booth overlooking the street known to younger generations as Love Lane. Their faces glow in the candlelight. He hands her a small gift box, and she opens it to reveal a beautiful gold locket, engraved with a heart on the back. They kiss in this café filled with young people showing their affection for one another.

Babak was once again deep in thought. David could see the cloud of sadness casting a shadow on his brother's face.

"What are you thinking about now, Babak?" David asked.

"I was reflecting on my tumultuous life and considering Rafeegheh, who stood by me when I needed a friend. Yet ultimately, I broke her heart. I was a mess, dealing with a broken heart of my own. Naturally, I skillfully concealed my pain and suffering from everyone. I lied and placed the blame on everything to disguise my feelings and my relationship with our tenant, Roya. Regardless, I haven't shared this with anyone."

Chapter 19

A Sad Farewell

It was a gloomy and depressing fall day in Tehran. It wasn't a good day to say goodbye to someone who loved you so dearly; in fact, it's never a good day to say goodbye to someone who loves you as dearly as Rafeegheh did.

Babak, a young man in his twenties, sat on a park bench in a quiet corner with Rafeegheh, who was the same age as him, lovely, and bubbly as ever. However, she had no idea that these few minutes with Babak could shatter her, leaving sadness lingering in her heart until she departed this unjust world, a heartache that would be buried with her under a mass of cold soil.

Babak's hair was a natural jet-black color, perfectly combed and held in place by the hairspray. The envy of many friends was so striking that girls constantly flirted with him. Not just girls, but even a few married women went beyond mere flirtation. He grew his mustache to cover a scar, a reminder of a little accident he had when he was just a boy.

Trying to look cooler than his peers, he wore freshly pressed blue jeans and a black T-shirt while holding a jean jacket in his hand. Many young men dressed this way; it was the style an American actor had worn in one of his movies.

Rafeegheh demonstrated a similar concern for her appearance. Her hair was beautifully styled in soft curls and set with a spray to maintain its shape. She wore a long floral skirt and a blouse that complemented everything else she had on. She mentioned feeling chilly, and Babak quickly draped his jacket over her shoulders.

After she heard what Babak had to say, Rafeegheh was upset, and her dark brown eyes were filled with tears.

Babak placed his arm around her, and she lay her head on his shoulder. His other hand held hers and pulled it to his lips, kissed it. She wiped a tear from her face with a handkerchief and whispered.

"Please take me with you. I cannot bear being without you. I will die here, you being so far away from me. I promise I won't be a burden; I'll go anywhere you want," She begged, as she fought back the tears.

"I won't ask for anything. If I have to, I will wash dishes or clean houses. We will have beautiful children together. You can choose their names; I know you mentioned you liked Farah. If we have a girl, you can name her after Farah, our queen, as you like, and if we have a boy, we can name him Arash, as you want to." She teared up.

Babak blinked through his tear-filled eyes. He whispered, "Please, Rafeegheh, I cannot allow you to put your life at risk for me. I'm ambitious and have big dreams. I don't know what I am going to do. I am leaving all my paintings that you love with you. Sell them or do with them as you wish. You know my family doesn't want any of them or to have anything to do with them. They always wanted me to be a doctor to save the lives of those in need. You will appreciate my painting more than anyone else. Please say it is okay for me to go."

She had a hard time saying it because she had a big lump in her throat and a heart full of sadness. But she gave in to him out of her love.

"Oh, God help me, please. If you think this is what you want, it will make you happy."

She felt a sick pain coming into her chest. It was as if water filled her lungs.

"I am so sorry, my love. Roya has broken your heart, hasn't she?" She whispered.

He sat there quietly, thinking about how she knew about Roya.

Rafeegheh kissed his hand.

"I have some savings; please let me give it to you. I do not want you to go through hard times," she said with broken words.

"No," he said with a big lump in his throat," he felt crushed by her unconditional love and care, and her offering him her savings, what he was doing in return, would haunt him for the rest of his life.

"I didn't know you could be so mean and cruel, breaking someone's heart so easily, especially hers; she was so kind and sweet. Our mother really liked her and was hoping that perhaps you might marry her. You are such a kind-hearted and caring person; you wouldn't hurt a fly," David said.

"I know. God has punished me in many ways because of my cruelty to her."

Babak sighs. Does our heart become callous after it has been broken so many times? Or do we become more empathetic and understanding towards other people's feelings?

"Anyway, David, I'm going to change the subject. I'm sure you remember Roya. She and her husband rented part of our house at the other end of the property. You were about fifteen; I was just eighteen when she moved out.

"Of course, I remember them. She was a teacher who always babysat us and helped us with our schoolwork," David said.

Babak continued in a somber voice, "I never imagined back when I was six years old, right after Nader's death. I helped mix the mortar and carry bricks for the workers to build our house, and that same house would be where I would lose my virginity and have my heart broken at the same time."

"When it all started, I was just fifteen, and Roya was twenty-five. I experienced the bittersweetness of love. I was so young, David."

"So, I was right. I suspected you weren't just getting help with your schoolwork. I once heard our parents talk about the two of you. They thought they should ask her to move out," David said.

"I see it wasn't entirely Roya's decision to move out, but ultimately, it turned out to be a good thing. I was addicted to her, and I often thought I would die without her in my life. After she left, there were many times when I considered taking my own life. When I think of her, I realize she was one of the best lovers I've ever had. Even now, thinking of her makes my heart tremble. In the end, she taught me how to be a great lover."

Chapter 20

Sweet Bitter Love

Roya was twenty-five, with long, light brown hair and creamy skin. She wore a skirt and blouse. She sat on the front steps of her apartment, which was situated at the end of the property, across from Babak's family living quarters, with Babak's painting studio directly below her apartment.

Babak, fifteen, handsome and athletic, with short hair, walked by Roya. He stole a glance at her perked breasts. Occasionally, he fantasized about touching them. "Damn, puberty!"

She looked up. "Hello," he said shyly.

"Hello, Babak. Are you going to your studio to paint?"

"Yes," Babak answered.

She slightly opened her legs for him to see. Babak couldn't help but take a quick look. He went down the steps to his basement studio and pulled out an unfinished nude painting from behind the other canvases leaning against the wall on the floor. He removed a torn nude female picture from a magazine from the back of the canvas and stared at it. He pinned it on the easel above the painting while playing classical music on his vinyl record player. He squeezed out a few colors on his wooden palette and, using his brushes, mixed several colors. He stared at the naked picture of a bust of a nude female, took a deep breath, and shook his head to distract himself from thoughts of Roya before starting to paint.

A few minutes later he heard a soft knock on the door.

"Who is it? Babak asked. The voice on the other side of the door said,

"It is I, Roya."

"Just a minute, please, Miss Roya."

He turned the painting around and hid the picture under his painting palette. Roya stood outside, where a creatively handwritten sign on the door read PRIVATE. Roya looked sexy in the low light, twirling her hair. The door cracked open. "Sorry to bother you, Babak. Can I borrow an onion, please? I will return it to you when I come back from the market later today," Roya said with flirtation.

"Yes. Do you want just one, Miss Roya?"

"Yes, please."

He stepped out, shut the door, and ran up the stairs. Roya waited for a minute, then entered the studio. She walked to the canvas and turned it over. She looked at the nude painting, astonished. Quickly, she turned the painting around, stepped out of his studio, softly shut the door, and waited.

"Oh, you bad boy." She whispers to herself with a grin.

Babak returned with an onion in his hand and went down the steps. He offered the onion to Roya, and their fingers brushed as she took it.

"Thank you. Babak, where are your mother and the kids?"

"They went to visit my aunt Mariam."

"Well, if you need anything, don't be shy. Do you need help with your studies today?" Roya asked.

Babak was nervous. "No, thank you. Is my music too loud?"

"No, sweetie. I like classical music. Can I see your studio someday?"

Babak shrugged.

After Roya left, Babak went to his easel and began working on his painting. Just a few minutes later, he stopped. He thought about how beautiful she was, then considered her husband, and shook his head to dispel the forbidden, evil thoughts.

He looked down and said, "Go away, stupid thing. You are going to get me into trouble someday." He left his studio and went out for a jog.

Babak sat shirtless at the table in the living room, deeply focused on his schoolwork. He heard a splashing noise, walked to the window, pushed the curtain aside, and peered out into the garden. Roya stood naked in a tub beneath a tree, partially obscured by tall flowers. She was washing herself. He caught sight of her breasts and part of her nude body. Babak gasped. He backed away from the window and sat at his desk. He pressed down on his arousal, looking painful. He glanced down.

"Go away! Dammit. You stupid thing."

"I thought she knew I was home. What the hell is she doing?" He spoke to himself.

A few days later, Moe, a sixteen-year-old cousin, and his best friend and wrestling buddy came by to visit Babak. They sat at Babak's desk.

"Is anyone home?" Moe asked Babak in a whisper.

"No, why?" Babak asked.

"One of my friends gave me a magazine to look at. His cousin brought it from Italy."

"The same guy who gave you those dirty magazines you talked about the other day?" Babak asked.

"Yes," he answered, then Moe opened the paper bag, took out the magazine, and showed Babak the cover. Moe had a big grin on his face.

"Oh shit, Moe," Babak said with his eyes wide open.

Moe flipped the pages and looked at Babak, looking at the pictures.

"What's wrong? You look pale. Are you already having a hard-on?"

110

"Shut up, Moe. If your father sees this magazine, you are a dead man."

"Why do you have both of your hands on the little Babak?"

"Shut up, Moe, and go. And take it with you." Babak said with a hoarse voice.

"I can leave the magazine here if you want; you can handle your big problem. I mean the little guy." Moe said with a smile.

"No, thanks, go and take the damn magazine with you."

"Okay, but I have a secret to share with you. It's a secret, so you can't tell anyone." Moe asked him.

"I promise."

"I had the best sex of my life last night. I worked on this rich, fifty-year-old, beautiful lady's Mercedes; she asked me to take it to her house after I fixed it. I drove it to her place last night, and she invited me into her beautiful home. She asked if I would like a drink, and I said yes. She then asked if I had ever had alcohol before. I replied that I was wondering if she had any whiskey. She said yes. Before I knew it, I found myself in her fancy bed. She is beautiful, and I think I am in love with her." Moe said.

"Yeah, right, dream on. Rich and beautiful lady," Babak said.

"I swear to God. She thanked me and said she might bring her car once a month to have a look at it. Honestly, Babak, and she was great—so much better than all those young girls. There are a lot more things to do in bed than just put it in and you are done," Moe said, shaking his head.

***

A week later, Babak's family was out visiting relatives. It was a hot day. He sat shirtless at his desk studying. American music was on. He heard a soft tapping noise on the windowpane. Babak walked over and brushed back the curtain. Roya stood outside the glass; she was wrapped in a towel, and part of her breast was exposed.

He opened the window "Hello, Babak," Roya said with a smile and lust in her voice.

"I ran out of soap. Could you check and see if you have an extra bar? If you do, can you please bring it outside to me?" She smiled and looked at his exposed chest.

She sometimes watched him from her room when he worked out in the yard.

"I will look," he said, his voice shaking. He glanced at her before walking away from the window. Closing his eyes, he tried to memorize her body so he could someday draw or paint her. He went to his closet, picked out a shirt, and put it on. Then, he entered the bathroom and looked at himself in the mirror. He gazed down at his penis and repeatedly muttered, "Go away, go away." He opened the cabinet, grabbed a bar of soap, and before going out to the yard, he walked to his desk and picked up a book. Finally, he stepped out into the yard.

"Stupid Moe, why did you show me those pictures?" he murmured.

Roya watched him approach her as she stood in the tub.. He held a bar of soap in one hand and a book in the other in front of his private. He walked to her slowly; the tall flowers obscured part of her body, and he stopped near Roya, not looking at her.

"Here, Mrs. Roya," he said.

She reached for the soap, but he was a bit too far.

"Come closer," she whispered.

He stepped closer to her. She grabbed the soap and his hand as well. His head was turned, and his eyes were closed. She stepped out of the tub, leaned forward, and kissed him on the cheek.

"You are too shy." She kissed him full on the lips.

He pulled back, startled. She looked at his book, smiled, and took a deep breath.

"Thank you, Babak. I have some cold soda for you to show my appreciation. If you'd like, you're welcome to come to my room later. I will be waiting for you," she whispered seductively.

He opened his eyes to thank her; she was standing naked in front of him. One hand covering her private parts.

"Sorry," he said. Then he looked at the flowers.

He turned and walked away, holding the book in front of him. Babak went to his bedroom and shut the door. He looked at himself in the mirror. He felt like a nervous wreck. He could hear his heart pounding a mile a minute in his spinning head as he combed his hair. "Why am I so fucking scared?" He spoke to his image in the mirror. He looked down.

"Go away, you fool. It's just a soda. Go back to sleep and don't wake up again, especially in front of her; that is disrespectful to a lady."

Roya was in a satin nightgown. She stood in front of the mirror, fixing her hair and applying makeup.

Babak tentatively knocked on her door. It slowly opened to reveal Roya standing in a radiant satin nightgown with part of her breasts exposed.

"Women are God's most fascinating creatures."

"Come in," she said.

The room was dimly lit, and the curtains were drawn. Classical music played on the vinyl record player. A lone candle glowed on the nightstand. Roya stood in front of her mirror, seductively applying lipstick. Roya looked at Babak in the mirror; she stopped and smiled.

"I am sorry, I did not know what to wear. I hope what I am wearing is okay," she told him while looking in the mirror. Then, she turned to face him.

"Are you sure your parents aren't coming back until late tonight? I don't want us to get caught. We'd both be in big trouble, and your parents would kick me out. We don't want that to happen, right?" she asked with a flirt.

"I'm sure, Miss Roya. They went to my uncle's house for supper," he said.

Babak sat nervously on the edge of her bed. The room smelled of her sweet perfume. She walked over to an ice chest and leaned down. Babak gazed at her exposed thighs. His heart began pounding.

She opened the ice chest, retrieved a bottle of soda, opened it, and then turned to walk toward him. Roya pressed the bottle against her cheek.

"Hmm, it feels good on a hot day. Thank you for coming over. I get lonely here some days."

She looked at him and seductively placed her lips around the mouth of the bottle. She tilted her head back and drank. Then, she sat next to Babak and offered him the bottle.

"I hope you don't mind my germs," she said.

Babak shook his head. She handed him the bottle, and he took a drink before passing it back to her. She sniffed his neck.

"I like your cologne," she said.

"I bet you have many girlfriends. You must have at least one," she said after his silence.

Babak looked at her and shrugged his shoulders.

"Have you kissed her yet? Oh, I know you have. What a lucky girl," she said again after his silence. She put her hand on his face. She turned his face. He looked at her, then looked at the floor, his hands between his legs.

"I noticed that you have started shaving. I've observed many things about you. Sometimes, I watch you when you

114

work out in the yard. You have a great body." She kissed him on the cheek. He was nervous.

"I wanted to give you a special fifteenth birthday gift the other day, but I couldn't give it to you then, so I'll give it to you today. I hope you'll like it."

He looked at her. She took a drink.

"Don't worry about anything. My husband is not coming back. You see, I could not bear him a child, and he has found a younger woman and divorced me. Promise me not to tell anyone, okay? If my school finds out that I am divorced, they will fire me, and if your parents find out, they will kick me out.

"I promise," he whispered. He brought his knees together, his hands resting on his manhood. Roya looked at him.

Of course, she was sure that he was ready. She placed her hand on his. She was extremely aroused and desperately in need of being loved. He could not understand any of this while his heart was pounding frantically in his head and an erection that he had never experienced before."

"Thank you for coming over. I want us to be friends. You know, like girlfriend and boyfriend. I want to stay here for a few years to save up some money so I can go to Shiraz to be with my family and buy a house there."

He sat there, not hearing a word she said. He felt sick to his stomach. The lust and desire burned all over her body. Unable to wait any longer, she stood up and urged him to get up, then held the bed sheet up and asked him to lie down on the bed. He obeyed. She lay down next to him and covered them both with the sheet. She straddled him and began to unbutton his shirt. He assisted her in removing it. He lay there nervously with his hands at his side, breathing heavily.

She kissed his lips, then his neck and ear. She then slowly moved her lips to his chest as she kissed him. Roya continued kissing and moving her lips lower and lower and closer to his aching manhood.

He arched his back and moaned. She removed his jeans and underwear, and she touched him.

"Oh boy, Babak, you are a big boy, you know," she whispered.

She lay on her back.

"You can be on top now to have your birthday gift," she told him.

She parted her legs. He lay on her. She helped the poor boy to enter her.

She kissed him on the lips. She placed his hand on her breast. They kissed more. They made short but intense love with her in control and him on top

He moaned and grunted, then shuddered but continued forcefully. After a long climax, he collapsed on her, and he breathed hard.

She kissed his neck. He lay on top of her, and she smiled.

"Oh boy, it looks like we can do it again. I like to be on top," Roya whispered.

They did it again. Both out of breath, they lay there for a while.

She took the bottle from the nightstand and offered him a drink. He sat, took a sip, and returned the bottle to her. She looked at him and smiled broadly. She finished the drink and placed the bottle on the nightstand. They lay in bed, holding hands and kissing. She thought about her husband and Babak and how intense and satisfying Babak was.

"Maybe you should go before your parents return." She whispered.

"Okay," he whispered. He felt half numb and half high.

He got out of bed in a way so she couldn't see his manhood. He bent to pick up his clothes from the floor.

"Please turn around before you put on your clothes, Babak. I want to see you. Do not be shy," she asks him.

He turned. She looked at him with a smile.

She kissed him goodbye at the door. "You are a man now. Sometimes you'll have to come here and stay overnight with me. But again, you must promise not to tell anyone about us. Not even your cousin Moe."

"I promise. Thank you for the amazing gift," he told her.

Babak went to his bedroom and lay on his bed, staring at the ceiling. His feelings were mixed, but guilt or not, forbidden or not, right or wrong, he liked what had happened. He felt exhausted, as if he were in one of his long wrestling matches. He took a deep breath, let it out, closed his eyes, and smiled. I am a man, he thought, and then he fell asleep.

After what happened that day, his life would not be the same again. He had no clue that heartbreak and pain were coming for him. The sex with Roya was like some kind of delicious drug that he tasted, and he would be addicted to for the rest of his life—the poor boy.

***

Babak and his family were sitting on the floor having dinner.

"Why don't you come with us, honey? I am sure your grandparents and cousins in the village would like to see you. We will be there only for two nights," his mother told him.

"It is going to be fun working at the farm, Babak," David said.

"No, Mother, I told you not this time. I have a couple of painting orders to finish, and I need to make a sign for the new beauty shop that is opening very soon. Father, it's okay for me to stay, right? I will stay with Cousin Moe at night."

His father nods his head, yes.

"Thank you, Father. I hope you have a safe trip. Don't worry about me."

***

117

Roya and Babak sat at a table, having dinner. She fed him with a flirty look and a smile. They ate, talked, laughed, kissed, and made love.

"Can I tell you something about kissing?" she asked.

He nodded. "Yes."

"I have read this in romance books. First, you should know that when a girl is ready to kiss, you'll know by the way she looks at you, and she will understand your gaze as well. You should slightly part your lips and kiss gently, allowing her to initiate the French kiss. If she is unfamiliar with it, ask if she would like to try. If she agrees and enjoys it, this is likely when she wants to make love. Of course, be mindful if she has not been with a man before. I will tell you more about having sex later."

Babak slightly opened his mouth and looked at her seductively.

"Yes," Roya said with a moan, then leaned over, and they kissed passionately and for a long time. He got up and carried her in his arms to her bed.

Roya and Babak made passionate love several times. They lay in each other's arms as Roya tenderly kissed him. She enjoyed being with him very much, particularly because he was more mature and respectful than most men. They fell asleep in her bed right above his art studio, where he had fantasized so many times about having sex with her. They repeated this the following night, sleeping in each other's arms once again.

In the early morning, Roya woke up and leaned over to kiss Babak gently as he slept.

Roya kissed Babak and shook him gently.

"Dear Babak, it's time to get up and go home before your parents return from their trip. And you need to get ready for school."

118

Babak grunted, "Okay." He got out of bed and got dressed. They kissed goodbye at the door. He went home and lay on his stomach on the floor.

His mother knocked on Babak's bedroom door.

"Babak, honey, it's almost ten. Why didn't you go to school? Are you okay?"

Babak grunted as he lay on the floor.

"Please, Mother, can you go to school and tell them I'm sick?"

"What do you mean, you're sick?" his mother asked, overly concerned.

"Mother, please go to school and tell them that I am sick. I do not feel good. I went out with Moe and had some raw liver and raw eggs as usual before our wrestling match. Maybe that made me sick."

He talked, pretending to be sick. Starting today, more pretending and lying will follow. One thing this family did not do was lie and steal.

His mother shook her head.

"Okay, honey. I will make you some soup after I get back."

"Thank you, mother," he said in a raspy voice.

He felt guilty and ashamed about lying to his mother; this would not be the last time he would lie and hide his and Roya's forbidden relationship and love affair. Their romance and bed-sharing continued for several years, and his love for her grew stronger day by day. He was behaving unusually, often blaming everything on his teachers and schoolwork.

Babak's parents lay in bed. Tamara whispered to Esrafil, "I am going to ask Roya to move out. Babak is a man now. I am not saying that something is happening between them. I trust him, but we have to be careful. I know he really likes Rafeegheh. He admires her so much. I asked Babak if he would marry Rafeegheh, and he said maybe."

119

Esrafil whispered, "I agree. We should have asked her to move out a long time ago. Talk to her nicely. She has been very helpful with the children's schoolwork."

"I will. Roya has mentioned a few times that she might want to go back home. She said that her husband moved to Kuwait and opened a clothing shop there, but she does not want to move there. She asked me not to tell anyone about this."

***

Babak, now eighteen, sat on a chair and painted the gorgeous 28-year-old Roya, who posed for him. Her long, curly hair covered her left breast, and gold fabric draped over her legs. Her hand gently rested on her right thigh.

"How was work yesterday?" Babak asked, looking up at the details of her face as he continued painting. Roya held her pose.

"You get more beautiful every day, Roya," he whispered.

She stared at him, unsure how to tell him she was leaving.

"The school is the same, but I am so tired of those spoiled students. I am considering transferring to another school or returning home You cannot show this painting to anyone, right, Babak?" she asked him.

"I promise, your work is so close. Besides, all the kids behave that way these days."

"We'll see. How is your beautiful study partner, Rafeegheh? Hopefully, she won't come between you and your college."

"Wait a minute. Why are you changing the subject? And what do you mean, we'll see?" he asked with an intense look.

Roya thought of Tamara asking her to move out.

"I will talk to you about that later. But for now, let's talk about your friend for a moment. I believe your feelings for her go beyond friendship and being study partners. Have you two had sex yet?"

"No, we are just friends. But I think she is falling in love with me. I keep saying we are just good friends, but the other day she whispered, 'I love you, Babak.' She is genuinely a nice person, and I like her a lot; I respect and admire her deeply, but that is all. She is too good for me. You're right; I need to keep my future in mind. I mean our future," Babak told her.

Roya stood and stared at him for a moment in thought.

"Tell me what is going on. Is something wrong?" he asked.

"Are you upset because she said she loves me?" he asked.

She shook her head, walked to him, straddled him on his chair, and wrapped her arms around him.

"I want to tell you something, but I need you to promise not to get upset.

Okay?" She said emotionally.

"I must—she pauses. I must return to Shiraz to be with my family soon and buy a house there."

"What do you mean? Go back to Shiraz? Just like that?"

Babak swallowed a lump and looked her in the face.

Roya brought her hands to his face and kissed him.

"We both knew this moment would come, and I am glad we had our time together. You are very smart, and you have a great future ahead of you. I am happy that you have a friend like Rafeegheh and that she will be there for you."

After Babak's silence, she continued.

"I am sorry I didn't tell you sooner. I did not want to see you suffer over the grief of my leaving any longer than you had to. This hurts me more than you could ever imagine. Please do not disclose anything about our relationship to anyone. Besides, I'm unable to have a child, which would be unfair to you." Roya told him.

"Fuck it, fuck the child. I don't give a damn for children," he said under his breath.

121

"Please, please don't be like this," she begged.

She leaned into him, kissed him, and hugged him closely.

"Remember? We talked about this so many times," she whispered.

He closes his eyes, and the paintbrush drops from his hand to the floor. He opened his eyes. His eyes were filled with tears.

"I know, but I didn't think I would fall in love with you the way I love you. Let me go with you, please. I love you, Roya. Please, do not do this to me." He begged her desperately.

"What about your family and friends? You know, in everyone's eyes, this is very wrong. We can't do this. I am so sorry. My mother always said that life goes on, and it must. You will learn that time heals everything, she whispered.

He wiped the tears with his hand.

My brother will be coming next Friday with a truck..."

Upset, Babak said, "Why did you flirt with me? Why did you make me fall in love with you? You needed to get fucked, and you used me. Why? Why me? I was just a fifteen-year-old boy. A boy. Why me? I will hate you for the rest of my life. Hate you, Ms. Roya. I am done with the painting; I will burn the damn painting, so I will not see your face again. You should leave my damn studio now."

Roya choked with teary eyes. "I am deeply sorry. Please don't say that. Yes, it was all my fault, but I love you. Please say you do not mean all that you said. How could you hate me after all those times together?"

He placed his face in his hands and wept. She held him in her arms.

"I am sorry, I did not mean that," he whispers in broken words.

She stood, kissed his head, and left the studio as he wept. She went to her room and lay on the bed where she had made love passionately and wept. In her heart, she truly had fallen in love with him.

She thought that if they had lived in a different time and place, she would have married him.

***

The moving day finally arrived. Roya stood before Tamara, Babak's mother, and spoke. "Mrs. Tamara, I am all packed, and everything is loaded into my brother's truck. The apartment is clean and ready for your next renter if you want to rent it," she said.

"You all were like a family to me. Especially you, Mrs. Tamara, you were like a mother, and Mr. Esrafil was always so kind. The children were like my own siblings. This is extremely hard for me," Roya said, choked and with a truth in her heart.

"You were like a daughter to me. You were so helpful with the children, watching them and helping them with their schoolwork, especially Babak. We will miss you, my dear Roya. You must promise to come back and visit us," Tamara said.

"I will. Where are the children? I want to say goodbye to them."

"The children are at their cousin's birthday party. Babak packed some food and gear and left for the mountains very early this morning. He said he and his cousin, Moe, plan to camp there for the night. He said to tell you, thanks for everything."

"I wanted to say goodbye to the children and wish Babak good luck. Please kiss the children for me; I will miss them." Roya hugged Tamara and thought of Babak as she sobbed on her shoulder. Then they kissed each other on the cheeks and said goodbye.

***

123

Babak looked at David, who was looking at him, as they sat on the bench outside the coffee shop near the museum on the crowded streets of Thran, Iran.

With all these events that have happened in my life so far, two things are embedded in my mind: our dear brother Nader's death and Rafeeghen's love for me.

"Of course, Roya always would have a special place in my heart because of the great sex we had. Sarah and I had some great times together, but in the end, she ruined everything. Because of her, I will no longer fall in love again."

"All these years, you have kept this secret from me. Wow." David said.

Chapter 21

The Innocent Victims

Traffic clogged the street. Cars, trucks, motorcycles, and people were everywhere. So was the thick pollution, which has caused many people to die because of breathing it in. Babak searched for a cab from the curb; he was impeccably dressed. A leather shoulder bag hung from his shoulder as he waited. Where he stood was only a block from his family home and a block from their famous bakery—a great neighborhood. His family was forced to sell the shop to an influential person in the government; in fact, more than half a dozen businesses were forced to sell, or their owners would be killed.

He looked around and saw beggars of all ages, both young and old, male and female. He noticed people picking up plastic bottles from the street or the filthy creek, where rats scurried everywhere. He observed individuals searching for food in trash cans or dumpsters. The suffering of the innocent does not end here.

Once, Tehran was regarded as one of the cleanest and most beautiful cities in the world, and I should also note that it was one of the most visited countries globally. But now, garbage is everywhere. Massive rats have overrun the city, just like the stinky and lazy mullahs; they are omnipresent. They are well cared for by the government, while many educated people are unemployed and live in poverty. He empathizes with the people, feeling helpless and hopeless. He stood there, numb. He was distracted by a young woman.

A cute young girl in her early twenties, heavily made up, approached him.

"Hello, Sir. Excuse me, can you please tell me where the Friday bazaar is located?" she asked with an accent.

125

"Hello, yes." He pointed. "Straight down that way, go six blocks. Turn to your right and go down half a block; you will see it."

Babak sensed her strong and cheap perfume.

"Is it safe for me to walk that far alone?" She spoke hopelessly, her face worn with fatigue.

"Just watch your purse and the traffic. It will take you ten to fifteen minutes on foot," he said.

"Actually, I don't feel safe walking by myself, men bother me, and I don't have any money for a taxi. If you're heading that way, may I please catch a ride with you?"

Babak felt sorry for her and understood her situation, which was caused by the government. He agreed to let her ride with him. If a cab ever stopped for them. They stood and waited quietly in a busy street in the big city. Finally, a taxi stopped.

The taxi driver leaned down and asked, "Where to?"

"The art museum," Babak told him.

The driver told them to get in. They sat in the back seat. After a few minutes, Babak leaned forward and started the conversation.

"What a mess. I don't know how you drivers do it," Babak said.

The cab driver had his head back and eyes on the road.

"Out of necessity, sir, believe it or not, I am an engineer. No jobs, sir. No jobs. People are tired of this situation, but who can dare to say anything? There are so many suicides and so many killings by the government," the cab driver said.

The cab driver honked a few times at the cab ahead of him as the young girl sat quietly.

"Damn idiots! Everyone wants to be a cab driver, but in the end, no one is making any money, and then some of them want to kill themselves," the cab driver said, looking out.

126

"One of my friends, who had just turned twenty-two, took her own life. She saw no future and no end to this mess. All while the leaders' kids go to America, drive Lamborghinis, and live in multi-million-dollar homes, while the rest of us suffer here," the young girl said. Looking at Babak and shaking her head.

"I do not know what to say, other than feeling heartbroken for the poor people," said Babak.

They sat quietly, gazing out, watching the crowd, and listening to the noise.

***

Babak and the young girl stood on the sidewalk.

"Thank you, sir. I want to know if I can spend the day with you. Maybe we could grab a bite after you're finished with your business? I can wait at the coffee shop near the museum. I don't mind whether you're married or not."

Babak was disgusted.

"So, Miss, was this your plan all along? Married or not, I wouldn't go with you. Why didn't you ask for money from the beginning?"

The young girl was hurt.

"I am not a beggar, sir; I provide my services for money. What is the difference between me and the rich college girls who sleep with male students for pleasure? Because I am unfortunate and forced to do this, it makes me," she choked.

"I don't want your damn money. I am just one of the victims of this revolution. My father used to have such hopes for me and called me his little doctor. Now look at me, I am glad he is not here to witness this. He died in the damn Iran/Iraq war when I was in first grade. We didn't have any money, so my sister and I were forced to drop out of school. Well, I need to go and make money to pay my share of the rent and help my sick mother with her medication. This is my last resort. Bye."

Babak was saddened.

"I apologize if I offended you. I did not mean that."

"You didn't, besides, I am used to being treated like trash. Sorry... I hate Iranian men; they are pigs. But you are different. Last night I was cheated by three Basigees. All night, they had their way with me, each taking their turn repeatedly until morning," her eyes filled with tears.

"They did not pay me a cent, and I could do nothing about those guys. They are given the green light to do anything, including raping and killing innocent people. Sorry, sir, I need to go."

"Please, tell me how much your rent is, ma'am?" Babak asked.

"You don't have to worry about it: one hundred dollars, sir."

Babak pulled out some money and counted it.

"Okay, this is a loan. When you have a lot of money, please give it to someone who needs it. There is little extra for groceries." He handed the money to her.

She took the money, hugged and kissed him on the shoulder, wiped her tears, then hurried into the crowd and disappeared.

He stood on the busy sidewalk and looked around.

"What happened to my country?" he whispered. Then slowly walked towards the museum.

Chapter 22

Endurance

Babak entered the museum. Classical music played on hidden speakers.

Babak walked sadly and looked at the art in thought. He stopped and stared at an abstract painting.

The rule enforcer behind him said, "Hello again, Sir. You are back."

Babak startled, turned, and saw the rule enforcer dressed in nice colorful clothing and moderate makeup. She looked beautiful.

"Oh, hello," he responded.

"I hope you can see the entire exhibit today. I know that you left the museum yesterday before seeing all the art."

"Yes, you are right, ma'am," he said in a sad tone of voice.

"Is everything okay?" she asked.

"Yes. No," Babak responded.

"If I may be of any assistance, please let me know," The rule enforcer said and continued. "I am sorry about yesterday if I caused you to leave. I hope you understand."

"Yes, I understand, but I should apologize for my inappropriate behavior. I am sorry."

"It's okay; there's no need for an apology. If you have any questions, please don't hesitate to let me know." She told him.

"Thank you. Are you knowledgeable about all the artwork here?" He asked.

"Fairly, is there something that has you puzzled?" she asked.

"Perhaps later I may have a question."

Babak looked her up and down, noticing that her makeup was artfully applied, making her look much more beautiful than she had the previous day.

"The way you are dressed tells me that you are some kind of artist. Am I right?" he asked.

"Kind of, you see that from my attire?" she asked.

"Yes, the color coordination is perfect, and it complements your beauty.

"Thank you. Are you flirting with me, sir?" she asked with a little smile.

"No, I'm sorry. Is it also illegal to compliment here? Compliments are very common in some countries."

"No, I guess not."

"Good. I do not want to be kicked out again."

"I will not kick you out. You, yourself, look like an artist. Are you, sir?"

"Yes, I am. Kind of."

"I thought so. Do you have any pictures of your work in your bag?"

"Yes."

"May I please see one, if you don't mind?"

"Of course you may."

He unsnapped the flap on his shoulder bag, removed a brochure, and offered it to her. She looked at his hand as she took the brochure, noticing he wore no ring. She is surprised.

After examining his art and reading part of his biography. She said, "Your art is wonderful, Mr. Babak. May I keep this? I would like to share it with my co-workers and my boss."

"Yes, certainly, Miss. I am flattered."

She looked towards the end of the lobby and saw a young lady approaching, and she smiled at her.

"That is my sister, Mehri," she told him.

Mehri, in her twenties, is petite, covered in her beautiful Montour and a scarf, and she walks with a spring in her step. Mehri smiled at her sister.

When she got closer, she said, "Hello, Sherin."

"Hi Mehri, Glad you could come."

They hugged and kissed each other on the cheeks.

"This is my sister Mehri," Sherin introduced her to Babak. Then she added, "This is Mr. Babak. He is an artist. I believe he lives in America. Look at his work." Sherin handed the brochure to her sister, Mehri. She held the brochure up and looked at it.

"Oh my God, these are amazing paintings, Mr. Babak. It's an honor to meet you," Mehri and Babak shook hands.

"We must invite Mr. Babak to our house as I think he would appreciate seeing our art collections," Mehri suggested to Sherin.

Sherin looked at Babak and said, "he is welcome to come over."

"Would tomorrow afternoon work for you? We will all be home." Mehri asked Babak.

"If it is okay with Miss Sherin," he said, looking at her

"Yes, that would be delightful," Sherin said as she looked at Babak.

"Good, please join us for coffee after you're finished here. We plan to go there later. You like coffee, right?" Mehri asked him.

"Yes, I do," Babak replied.

"Well, I should go to my job," Sherin said.

***

Later, they all walked to the coffee shop, which was only one block from the museum. The host welcomed them and directed them to the booth where they usually sit. They sat in a booth in the crowded coffee shop, and drank coffee, dessert, and conversation. After half an hour, Mehri stood and grabbed her purse.

"I would love to stay longer. I enjoyed the conversation, but I need to be somewhere. I will see you tomorrow, Mr. Babak," she said.

Babak stood, bowed, and said, "It was very nice to meet you, Miss Mehri."

"Mr. Babak, it was my pleasure." She turned and walked away. Babak sat and looked around, thinking about the stark contrast between the people inside the cafe and the poverty outside. Here, the price of one cup of coffee is the cost of living for one day for a family. Babak and Sherin were in awkward silence in a crowded coffee shop as they munched on their dessert.

Sherin broke the silence by asking Babak if he came from a big family in Tehran.

"Yes, I come from a large family," he answered.

"Can I ask a personal question?" Sherin asked him.

"Yes, you may."

"Are you married? I do not see any rings on your fingers."

"Not anymore. My wife wanted her freedom and her kids - I mean, our kids. It's a long story, and I do not want to bore you with it today. How about you?" he asked.

She shook her head, no. She showed her fingers.

"Like you, not anymore. I, too, do not want to bore you," she said.

Babak placed his hand on hers.

"If you want to share your story, I would love to listen."

"No, you would not love it," she looked down at his hand on top of hers.

She suddenly pulled her hand away from his and got up and hurried from the coffee shop. Babak sat there for a minute in thought, then he got up and rushed out of the coffee shop. He raced up behind her on the crowded sidewalk.

"Miss Sherin, please wait," he whispers behind her. Sherin hesitated next to a tree out of the pedestrians' way. Babak stood in front of her.

132

"I am sorry if I said or did anything to offend you. I want to apologize," he apologized in her silence. He asked her if she was still okay with him going to her house.

"Mehri invited you; I ---"

A ten-year-old flower vendor girl approached and interrupted her.

"Sir, would you like to buy a rose for your beautiful wife? It's only $1.00 a rose. Please, kind sir, would you?" the flower vendor said, taking Babak's hand and shaking it, as if begging.

Babak looked at her, smiled, and nodded yes.

"Yes, young lady, I will take them all if that's okay," he asked her.

"All six?" the young flower vendor with big, dark eyes asked.

"Yes," he answered.

"Thank you, kind Sir," the girl said. Sherin watched as Babak pulled out a $10.00 bill and handed it to the girl.

"Give my beautiful wife one rose and keep the change; the rest of the flowers are yours as well."

The flower vendor took the money and passed a rose to Sherin.

"Your husband is a nice man. I hope that you two live together for a long time. Wow, $10," she said.

She walked to a man sitting on a cardboard on the sidewalk. The man's head was down, and his hand was open.

The 10-year-old flower vendor delivered the good news to the man.

"Father, a man gave me $10.00 for only one flower," she told him.

Her father looked at her, nodded, smiled, and took the money.

A handwritten sign, taped to the wall behind him, read, "Kidney for sale."

Selling a kidney or any organ has become a common event to make money to survive in Iran. Suicide is quite common among adults and young children in Iran due to poverty and government pressures.

Although Sherin knew that Babak or anyone else did not have an answer to her question, she still asked him: "Is there such a thing as a happy life? Thank you for the beautiful rose. You are welcome to come to our house if you still want to. Can we go to the coffee shop and start over?" she asked.

He looked at her and nodded yes.

***

Sherin and Babak returned to the coffee shop and sat in the same booth. A portion of their dessert and cold coffee were still there. The coffee shop was busy and well-to-do, with happy men and women talking and laughing around them.

Sherin reached into her blouse and pulled out a locket. She opened it and showed him a tiny picture inside. He looked at the picture and the locket. The locket seemed very familiar to the one he had given to his girlfriend a long time ago. It was the same locket. Then he saw the engraved little heart on it, which made him sure.

"This is a photo of my adorable daughter, Mahsa. She was only seven years old when..." She choked up and then put the locket back into her blouse.

"I was in college that day when Meri called me. She asked me to go to the hospital right away. My husband had picked Mahsa up from school. He was high on some drugs. I was too late to say goodbye to my daughter." Sherin looked down sadly. She took a sip of water.

"It was all my fault," she whispered.

With much sympathy, Babak asked, "Why do you say that, Miss Sherin? No, it was not your fault at all if he was

134

driving under the influence. Please, you should never blame yourself; that can only put more burden on you."

She looked down and shook her head.

"My mean husband died as well," she looked at Babak and continued.

"If I had picked her up, that would not have happened. I still would have her with me. People say she is in heaven among the angels. I just hate that; I do not give a damn about the made-up angels and heaven. I want my daughter here with me in my arms."

Babak looked at her beautiful, sad face.

"Am I boring you, Mr. Babak?" she asked with her soft, sweet, and lovely voice.

"No, not at all. Please continue if you wish... Sometimes, it helps to talk to a good friend or a caring stranger." Babak told her.

"My soul was stolen from my life. We were so happy; she and I always came here for dessert. She loved the cream puffs here so much. I stopped going to college. I lay in bed for months, in my tears and sorrow. If it were not for my sisters and my mother, I would not be here today."

"I am so sorry for all your pain, Miss Sherin. The kind and caring people get hurt the most," Babak told her. "I am glad you are still here."

"My husband was the worst thing that came into my life. He crushed me. Once, I told him that I didn't marry him because I loved him; I married him because my father and brother forced me to. For that reason, he always beat and abused me. My poor, blessed mother was not there to stand up for me. However, Rafee, an old friend of ours whom we affectionately call our mother, has always been there for us. She raised us. She is such an Angel and has gone through so much pain and agony in her life. Oh, Mr. Babak, life is so cruel. This country has been cursed since the takeover by these evil religious people."

She held her coffee cup in trembling hands and then put the cup on the table.

Babak nodded while his eyebrow was raised.

"I do understand your hurt and suffering about your poor daughter. I lost my dear brother in a freak accident when I was only five, and Nader was only eight years old. He was my best friend, and we were always together. Our family was devastated. My mother and I did not eat for many days, and because of that, I almost died."

"I'm glad that you did not die. Please tell me what happened," Sherin asked, looking concerned.

"My thirteen-year-old uncle Ali kicked hard in Nader's private area; he died a few days afterward. Later, I realized that I was causing additional stress and pain to my poor parents."

"How so?" she asked.

"I was disappearing for hours. And that was causing fear and stress for my parents, especially for my mother. To end that, one day my mother burned the bottom of my foot with a hot spoon, which I always think I deserved, but she felt bad about it and cried. That stopped me from going too far from our home."

"Your mother must have loved you a lot," she said.

"After my brother's death, she was so worried about me getting hurt that any time I had a little cold, she would rush me to the doctor. "She probably kissed me a hundred times a day," he said.

"I would have done the same," Sherin said.

"Should we get more coffee?" he asked.

"No, I'm okay. Too much coffee doesn't agree with me later in the day," she said with a smile.

"Do you know what? Miss Sherin, you have such a beautiful smile, and I'd like to see more of it."

" I will try to smile more when I am with you, and I like your smile as well."

She placed her hand on his. "We should get going. Did you drive?" Sherine asks him.

"No, I took a taxi."

"Then, I will give you a ride," Sherin told him.

"Miss Sherin, you should not give a ride to a stranger."

"My instinct tells me I can trust you," she said, looking right into his eyes.

"I hope that your instinct is correct."

She gave him a warm smile.

They talked on their way to Babak's home, and they both seemed anxious to meet again. She kissed him on the cheek goodbye.

"Thank you, Babak," she told him.

"I had a great time, Sherin. And thank you for the ride in your nice car."

***

Babak went home, after talking to the family and having dinner, grabbed a cup of tea, went to the garden, and sat there thinking. He thought about Sherin and how kind and beautiful she was. He decides that she is not the kind of woman he wants to have casual sex with. He couldn't decide whether to go to her house or not. There was something else, besides her classiness, that attracted him to her. Maybe she would make a good friend? "One more visit, then I will know." He convinced himself. "Perhaps I will ask her where she got that locket."

***

Sherin went home and wanted to call Babak, but she thought it would be better to wait. As usual, she took her old family friend, Rafee, whom she affectionately called "mother," into the garden. Rafee is in her late forties, is neat and elegant, with white hair. She sat in her wheelchair as Sherin pushed. Rafee reached for Sherin's hand. A sign that reads "THE ART STUDIO" hangs above the door of a cozy brick building in the background

"He seems kind, gentle, and has values that a man can't fake. On the second day of seeing him, I opened my heart to him. Mehri told me she thought he was nice; in fact, Mehri invited him over. He is very handsome, but a little older than I am. He may be ten or fifteen years older, about the same age gap as Ray and Farah. I gave him a ride home," Sherin told her mother.

Rafee turned and looked at her. "You did? Oh, my dear. I see happiness in your face and your eyes. Just be careful; it is a dangerous world. It is hard to find a good and honest man these days. He's a lucky man to have met you. I can't wait to meet him."

"I hope he shows up. I told him a little about Father. I wanted him to know before he heard from someone else. I want you to tell me, please, what you think of him if he comes."

"I will, dear. You need a good friend. Maybe we should prepare a nice meal tomorrow night."

"That would be good, Mother. I don't know why I feel so nervous."

"He must have impressed you," Rafee told her.

Chapter 23

The Love Child

It was nearly dusk, and David and Babak sat in David's car in front of a vast, ornate steel gate. David ran his fingers through his hair, looking upset. He tried to change his brother's mind about going to Sherin's house.

"I have a bad feeling about you going into this house. This house belonged to the Pahlavi family. An evil member of the Supreme Court confiscated it and gave it to his children. Please, Babak, forget about her and let's go home or somewhere to eat." David practically begged him not to go into that house.

"You worry too much. The man's kids are different. Sherin told me a little about her father and her family. She seems honest and kind, and she wouldn't have invited me to her house if I were in danger. I like her, David."

"You like every beautiful woman you see. Did she tell you why and how her younger brother disappeared?"

"No."

"That was her own father's order, because he was causing too much trouble for him, and he also killed his wife," David said.

"What a fucking evil. I promise I will be very careful," Babak said.

"If it is sex that you want, there are plenty of women out there who would sleep with you, few of them you know," David said.

"I do need sex, but I do not like to just jump into bed with anyone. I needed to get to know the woman first. After only two conversations with her, I realized that I liked her and wanted to know more about her. She and I can be friends. I can have sex with different women."

"Okay, go ahead. But be careful. You should know that if you sleep with her and her father finds out, you're a dead man, and I can't do anything about that," David warned his brother.

"Whatever is written on my forehead or whatever my fate is, do not worry," Babak said.

Babak got out of the car and walked toward the tall, decorative steel gate, holding a bouquet and a gift box. He rang the bell and waited.

The gate slowly opened, revealing a tall, bearded man in his thirties.

"Hello," Babak said.

"Hello, sir, come in," the man responded. Babak stepped inside as the man shut the gate. He followed the man and admired the beautiful garden, the pool filled with large goldfish, and the flowers surrounding the pool. Babak followed the man up the porch in front of a stunning brick mansion.

"Please wait here. Someone will be with you soon, sir."

Babak sat on a patio chair, placed the flowers and the gift box on the table, waited, and looked around.

The front door of the mansion opened, and Sherin stepped outside wearing a short skirt and a blouse. Her long, curled, light brown hair flowed freely, and she looked radiant in the sunset light.

"Welcome, Mr. Babak."

"Hello, Miss Sherin."

He stood as she approached, and they shook hands. Mehri, dressed in shorts and a blouse, entered the patio and smiled at Babak.

"Hello, Mr. Babak. I am glad you could make it," Mehri said with a welcoming smile.

"Hello, Miss Mehri, good to see you."

140

"Good to see you too, Babak. Sherin, are you two coming into the house soon?" Mehri asked.

"No, I am going to give Mr. Babak a quick tour of the garden and the studio before it gets too dark."

"If that's okay with you, Mr. Babak?" She asked.

"I would like that. Thanks."

"Dear Mehri, could you please take Mr. Babak's gifts into the house, and bring us something to drink?"

"Yes, I will, Sherin."

Babak followed Sherin into the garden. She stopped, looked at Babak, and pointed to a flower.

"This flower is extremely rare and grows only here in Tehran. They can be found in those mountains." She points toward the nearby mountain. And Babak stared at it.

"I was not sure if you would come. I was hoping."

"I wanted to, but I had mixed feelings," Babak confessed.

"I am happy that you came," she said in a soft and sweet voice.

"Good. So am I. The flowers are so beautiful. Now I remember seeing them there, in those mountains."

Babak stared at the mountain as they walked.

"Are you indulging in an enjoyable recollection of your past?" she asked.

Babak grinned as he looked back at her. "Yes, I am. The good old days are all I have to say." He thought of the times he spent there with Roya and Rafeegheh.

"Mother often talks about the good old days, how wonderful life was then, all their freedoms, and how much she loved the mountain. Almost every day, she sits by her window having tea, reading books, writing poetry, and gazing at the mountain. It seems like she is waiting for some miracle to happen."

Mehri walked towards them, holding a bottle of red wine. A young, beautiful (20s), with short, deep brown hair, and a dark-eyed

141

girl, carried two wine glasses, accompanying Mehri. They approached Babak and Sherin.

"Mr. Babak, this is Farah, our dear friend and sister. Farah, this is Mr. Babak. The artist I told you about."

Babak stared at Farah, shocked to see her.

"Nice to meet you, Miss Farah," Babak said.

Babak extended his hand to shake hands with Farah.

"It is nice to meet you, Mr. Babak. They were right when they said you were a handsome man."

Farah and Babak release their hands. Farah held the wine glasses up, and Mehri poured the wine.

"I hope that you like red wine," Sherin said.

"I do," he said.

Farah handed a glass to Sherin and one to Babak.

"Thank you, Miss Farah, and Miss Mehri," Babak said.

"You are welcome. Please excuse us; we need to go in to help get ready for dinner. See you two later," Mehri said, then gave the bottle to Sherin.

Babak walked side by side with Sherin, looking at the ground in thought. Something about Farah reminded him of an old friend.

They approached an old brick building, and a hand-crafted sign hung above the door that read "The Art Studio." She opened the door and offered Babak to go in first. They entered the studio, and Sherin shut the door. Babak walked around holding his wine glass as the sunset filtered into the room. He examined the studio, which was filled with easels and tables of finished and incomplete paintings and drawings.

"These are nice, Miss Sherin," he complimented.

Sherin leaned against the closed studio door, the warm light making her look even more beautiful. She held her empty wine glass, admiring Babak with sleepy eyes.

He looked at her, and his heart trembled. She looked irresistible.

Now is a good time to leave this room if he does not want to have sex with her. If he stays, he might ruin everything.

He walked to the window and looked out. And wondered what if she is good in bed? Shit, I think I am drunk. It's best if I get out of here.

Sherin was tipsy.

"The paintings are not all mine. We have a painters' group here. They are mostly beautiful young girls. You should come... and share your knowledge with us."

Babak finished the rest of his wine and approached her. He took her empty wine glass, walked to the table near the window, and placed it next to the empty bottle.

"Did you say young and beautiful? I'll definitely come," with a flirty look and a smile, he said.

Wine definitely played a role in her behavior.

Sherin couldn't take her eyes off him. And she smiled.

"Can I ask you something if you don't mind? Please be honest with me, Mr. Babak. Okay?"

Babak unconsciously stepped closer to her and looked at her.

"You would know when a girl wants to be kissed." This is what Roya told him a long time ago.

"I can't believe we finished the whole bottle," she said drunkenly.

"That was not a question," Babak said.

"Really?" She shook her head and smiled.

"Why did you return to the museum the next day?" she asked.

Babak looked into her mesmerizing eyes.

"Miss Sherin, if I say or do anything stupid please slap me and tell me to leave."

"I will," she whispered.

"I came back because I was looking for trouble," he said.

"Did you find it?" She asks.

"I am not sure yet," he said, staring at her.

He was sure that she wanted him.

She blushed, then she turned grave.

"It is so charming when a woman blushes for a man standing right in front of her," he told her, and then he blushed.

"Is it?" she asked in her sexy voice that he loved to hear.

"When you left the coffee shop, I was concerned that I would never see you again,' he confessed in a shaky tone of voice.

"Is that right?" Sherin asked.

"Yes," he answered.

"I swore on my poor mother's sweet memories and grave that I'd never again have a relationship with another man. But you have stirred a desire in me that I can't fight. I'm glad you came back," she told him.

Babak brushed her long hair behind her shoulder. She closed her eyes and tilted her head back. He gently kissed her neck, and she moaned. He moved his lips to hers. She ran her fingers through his hair, and they kissed hungrily. She stopped kissing and looked at him. Her heart beat frantically. He looked at her, waiting to see what would happen next. She ran her tongue on his lips, and soon their tongues touched. Her hands moved to his lower back, and she pressed herself into him with a moan. He had one hand on the back of her head and the other on her breast. They kissed hard. She opened her eyes slightly to look at him. Then she saw their guard outside the window, looking in. He hurried away as their eyes met. She abruptly pushed Babak away.

"I am sorry," he said in shock.

"No. It was not you. The damn guard saw us. He will report it to my father, which is not a good thing. Let's go to the house," She shook her head.

"Now I am worried about you," she whispered.

"Do not think or worry about it at all," Babak said.

It was dusk, and they walked toward the house. Soon, they entered the foyer where we could hear a violin playing. Sherin and Babak removed their shoes and placed them on a small Persian rug beside the door.

"Hello, Ray," Sherin calls out. Sherin and Babak walked to the guest room, and the music came to a stop.

Babak followed Sherin into a beautifully decorated room. A lush Persian carpet lay on the floor beneath a large crystal chandelier, and valuable paintings in ornate frames decked the walls.

Ray, a tall, skinny man in his late thirties with long, combed-back hair, sat on a stool beside a grand piano holding a violin in the family room.

On the floor nearby, Omeed (10), a handsome young boy, read silently. Sherin and Babak entered the family room.

"Mr. Babak, please let me introduce you to my brother, Ray," Sherin said.

Ray stood and put the violin down on the stool. He grabbed his cane. Babak walked to Ray and extended his hand out to him.

"It is nice to meet you, Mr. Ray," Babak said politely.

Ray ignored Babak and left the room with a dark look on his face. Babak looked after Ray. Sherin was embarrassed. Omeed stood.

"Mr. Babak, this is Omeed, the son of our housekeeper Fatemah," Sherin told Babak.

"Hello, Mr. Omeed, it is nice to meet you."

They shook hands.

"It is nice meeting you, sir," Omeed said.

145

"Omeed is a good boy, a great soccer player, and a chess player," Sherin told Babak.

"Really? I also played soccer; it's one of my favorite sports. Do you watch the games on TV?" Mr. Omeed.

"Yes, sir, almost every game."

"What is your favorite team, Omeed?

"Persepolis, Sir."

"Mine as well. Have you been to the stadiums to see any of the games?"

"No, Sir, but maybe someday. I hope."

"Babak placed a hand on Omeed's shoulder. Sherin watched them. Then she left the room. She went to her bedroom and shut the door. She leaned against the door. She took a deep breath and let it out.

"God dammit, Babak," she whispered. She shook her head and left the room. She walked to the family room. She stood and watched Babak and Omeed talk.

"I hear that Persepolis is going to play against another team. Maybe you and I should go to watch it. I'd like to see one. What do you say, Mr Omeed?" Babak asked.

Omeed looked at Sherin. She smiled and nodded, and Omeed turned to Babak with a grin.

"That would be so awesome, Mr. Babak. I will have to ask my mother first."

Sherin looked over to Babak in thought.

"That sounds good, Mr. Omeed. I do hope your mother agrees. and one of these days, we should play chess."

"Sounds good," Omeed said.

Sherin stood patiently and watched the two converse. She rubs Omeed's shoulder as she looks at Babak.

"Is he real? Or trying hard to get me into bed. But with his looks and charm, he can have any woman in Iran these days," she thought.

146

Rafee, a pale, beautiful woman with silver-gray hair and elegantly dressed in a pantsuit, entered the room in her wheelchair. Sherin approached her and kissed her on the cheek.

"Mr. Babak, this is my dear mother, Rafee. Mother, this is Mr. Babak," Sherin introduced.

"Welcome to our home. It is a pleasure to meet you, Mr. Babak," Rafee said in her soft, sweet voice.

"Thank you for having me in your beautiful home."

Mehri and Farah walked into the room.

"Dinner is almost ready. I hope you are all hungry. Fatimah has prepared a real feast," Mehri boasted.

"Would you all please excuse me for a minute? I'll go get Ray," Sherin said.

Sherin entered the porch and glared at Ray as he smoked, sitting on a bench under the porch light.

"What the hell was that? Why did you have to be so rude and such an ass to our guest?" she whispered angrily.

"Dammit, Sherin. Why did you bring home this fricking old man? Who is he, your boyfriend now?" Ray said, his voice laced with anger.

"Keep your voice down and don't even go there. First, he may be fifteen years older than I, but I am a widow, and what man would want to be with me anymore? Unless they have their eyes on our money. Besides, you have no room to talk; you and Farah also have a significant age gap."

"He is a nice and decent man," she said.

"You are a beautiful woman. You can do so much better than him."

"Oh, yeah? You know who would be good for me. Why don't you fix me up with one of your rich friends? Oh, I almost forgot. We have already tried that, haven't we? Such a nice guy, such a loving and caring man he was."

147

"Ray, I'm trying to forgive you and put the past behind us," Sherin continued, getting in his face with piercing eyes. She whispered, pointed her finger at him, and shook it. "My life has been hell so far. But from now on, I want to live the way I want and have fun. So, keep your nose out of my business. I can do whatever I want. I don't need your damn permission anymore. You had better come in and apologize to our guest for your rudeness. And I do not want any damn sarcasm, Ray," she told him.

Sherin strode to the door and tossed one last glare over her shoulder before she entered the home.

"It is time to eat," she told him.

Farah, Mehri, and Omeed were giving Babak a tour of the house, sharing details about the paintings in the collection. Babak examined the paintings while Rafee sat in her wheelchair watching them. Just then, Sherin entered, and Rafee turned to her. Sherin shook her head, walked over to Rafee, placed her hands on her shoulder, and began to massage it.

***

Everyone, including the housekeeper Fatimah, gathered around the large table, finishing a grand feast artfully presented on colorful, expensive China plates. Babak wiped his mouth with his napkin.

"Thank you, everyone, for this great meal and your hospitality. Especially Mrs. Fatimah and Mr. Omeed, the meal was superb," Babak complimented.

"Thank you, Mr. Babak. I am glad you liked the food," said Omeed.

"Mr. Babak, how do you feel about being back in Iran? Has it changed much since your last visit?" Farah asked.

"My last visit was ten years ago. Everything has changed significantly, and unfortunately, for the worse. Poverty deeply

148

saddens me. The way the government is managing the country and killing innocent people is alarming. The economy is struggling, and they are also destroying the country. Well, I hoped to come back to live here, but now I am uncertain," Babak said.

"If you decide to stay, we know many influential people, and I am sure we can find a teaching job at one of the universities," Sherin said.

Rafee quietly watched Babak from across the table.

"The man said he does not like the government," Ray told Sherin in a rude tone,

"You could teach private classes or have art shows. Your extraordinary talent could earn you a substantial income. I can arrange a show at the museum," Sherin told Babak.

"I am sure he can make his own decisions. He does not need anyone's advice. For God's sake, he is a grown man," Ray told Sherin.

Sherin glared at Ray and stormed out of the room. After an awkward moment, Farah, Mehri, Fatimah, and Omeed got busy clearing the table while Ray hobbled towards the porch.

"Dear Farah, could you please bring some tea for us?" Rafee asked.

"Okay, my dear Mother," Farah responded.

Farah left the room, and the others followed. Rafee and Babak were alone.

"Mr. Babak, may I ask how long you plan to stay?" Rafee asked.

"Five or six weeks, perhaps more," he answered.

"Sherin told me that you were an exceptional artist. May I ask what your last name is?"

Well, I...

At this time, Farah entered the room with a tray of tea and interrupted him.

"Mr. Babak, would you like sugar cubes or honey with your tea?"

Farah placed the tray on the table. She took one cup of tea to Babak and one to her mother.

"I would like a couple of sugar cubes, please," he responded.

At this time, everyone comes into the room. They all sat, having tea and dessert.

"Mr. Babak, where did you go to school in Tehran?" Rafee asked.

"The Tehran Technical School and Monir Night High School."

Rafee's hand shook as she held the teacup. She put it down on the table and stared at Babak incredulously. Farah left the room.

"There is no doubt. He is my love, Babak, but he does not recognize me. Oh, dear God. Sherin and Farah must never find this out," she thought.

Farah returned with two paintings. Then leaned against the wall behind Rafee.

"Mr. Babak, what do you think about these paintings? I forgot to show them to you earlier," Farah said.

Rafee turned and saw her portrait and the seascape painting.

Those were the paintings I gave to Rafeegheh before I left Iran. How did they end up with them?" he thought.

Everyone sat and talked, drank tea, and enjoyed their dessert.

Rafee placed her face in her hands. Babak stared at the paintings, numb with shock.

Sherin looks at Rafee with concern.

"Is something wrong, Mother?" Sherin asked in a very concerned tone because of her medical condition.

Everyone stared at Rafee. She shook her head, then placed her head on the table.

"What is wrong, Mother?" Farah asks worriedly.

Rafee shook herself with her face cupped in her hands. Ray stood, leaning on his cane.

"Farah, get her pills. Don't just stand there, get some water, Fatemah," Ray ordered both.

With Babak's suggestion, the girls helped Rafee onto the floor.

Rafee lay unconscious on the floor, and Farah wept as she held her mother's legs up.

Babak sat on his knees on the floor beside Rafee. Ray and Sherin stood over him. Fatimah held a glass of water, Omeed beside her.

Mr. Doctor, what the hell is this, holding her legs up? She should have her medicine," Ray spat.

"Does this happen very often, Miss Farah?" Babak asked in thought.

"Any time she is very upset," Farah said, distraught.

"Do not worry, Miss Farah, she will be okay."

"Have her doctors ever said anything about holding her legs up?" Babak asked.

Farah shook her head no.

"This often happens to a person with a weak heart, typically after experiencing a shock or receiving bad news. The person needs oxygen more than anything else. When you hold the legs up, more blood flows to the heart, helping them regain consciousness," Babak informed.

"Oh, my dear Babak, it is you," Rafee whispered.

Babak now realizes who she was; he felt her pulse. He teared up.

***

Babak had a flashback about the day he said goodbye to Rafeegheh in a park as they sat on a bench in a quiet area.

"Please, Babak, take me with you. I will die here with you, so far away from me," Lafeegheh begged with her eyes full of tears.

"God, please help me," she said, and wiped away her tears.

"I will give you my blessings, along with my life and my heart. Roya has broken your heart, hasn't she?"

Babak was quiet and stared at the grass in the park where he said goodbye to her.

"I have some savings. Please let me give it to you. I don't want you to go through hard times wherever you go," she said, choked up.

Babak stared at the ground. He shook his head no.

"I will be okay," he whispered.

They sat quietly for a minute.

"God damn you, Rafeegheh, why do you have to be so nice? Please do not make me hate myself even more."

***

Shortly after Babak left Iran, the Islamic radical group took over Iran, and they made people's lives hell, and this beautiful country was turned upside down.

***

We are back in Sherin's house after Babak's flashback.

Everyone watched Babak as he gazed at Rafee.

"Rafeegheh, are you okay?" Babak whispered.

A tear ran down her cheek.

"How do you know her real name? Farah asked, with anger in her voice.

Rafee took a deep breath.

"Oh, my dear Babak, you have returned, thank you, dear God," she said.

"You can put her legs on the floor now, please," Babak told Farah nicely.

Farah gently places her mother's legs back on the floor. They helped Rafee into her wheelchair as she stared at Babak. Babak stood there with a confused thought.

"Mother, what is going on? Who is this man, and how does he know your real name?" Farah questioned her mother.

"I tried to find you. I went to your sister's shop, and she said you'd moved on and were happy. I was happy for you. I didn't want to disturb you. Tell me, Babak, did you ever get the letter I wrote you? I gave it to your sister and asked her to make certain that you received it."

Babak shook his head no.

"Oh, poor dear," Rafee said.

Babak stared at her as he stood. Thinking about what has happened to her.

"This is the boy I loved so many years ago; I have been waiting to see him once more before I die."

Babak looked at Sherin, who had her eyes fixed on him, in deep thought.

"I have missed you. I can't believe it's you after all these years. How is this possible?" Rafee asked.

"Yes, Rafeegheh, it has been a long time." Babak closed his eyes and shook his head. Farah stared Babak in the face. Farah was angry at Babak.

"So, are you the jerk who abandoned my mother all these years?"

Suddenly, Farah swung at Babak and slapped him across the face. Babak looked down. She slaps him again.

"Farah, please stop," Rafee begged her daughter.

"You broke her heart and destroyed her life. Just look at her, this is all your fault." Farah said.

"I am terribly sorry, Miss Farah," Babak apologized.

Sherin stood, speechless. Fatimah and Omeed left the room while Farah pounded her fist on Babak's chest. He took it silently.

153

"Farah, please stop," Sherin told her in a stern voice.

"Ray, please stop Farah," Rafee urged, distraught.

Ray limped over to Babak with his cane.

"Get out of here, you son of a bitch. You have caused enough trouble. I did not like you from the moment I saw you." Ray yelled at Babak, then he swung his cane and hit Babak on the arm.

"Get out!" Ray yelled.

Babak stared daggers at Ray.

"Get out before I call the guard," Farah yelled.

"Enough, Farah; stop before you give Mother a heart attack," Mehri said.

Babak was anguished. He looked at Rafee and then at Sherin. He walked to his shoes and put them on. He then opened the door.

"Babak, wait. It's not safe; it's almost time for curfew," Rafee wept.

Babak shut the door before she finished.

Rafee begged everyone.

"Could someone please give him a ride home?"

"Sherin, please don't let him go like this. Please, I beg you, Sherin. Someone, please make sure he gets home safely," Rafee begged again.

"I am sorry, Mother. I do not know what to do," Sherin said.

   ***

Babak decided to walk home. After his ugly divorce from Sarah, Babak definitely did not need another blow in his life; right when he thought he might have met someone that he liked, this happened. "Will I see Sherin again, or try to forget about her?" Oh, my dear Rafeegheh, what happened to you?" There were so many things he needed to sort out. Like Sherin said, is there such a thing as happiness? Babak talked to himself as he walked in the shadows of the alley. He thought about his grandparents and their fate, as well as his own.

    ***

A black car with tinted windows pulled up to the curb. Two large men got out and approached Babak. Babak stopped.

What the fuck? Not now, assholes; I am going to kill you, bastards; this is all your fault, he talked to himself. It was you guys who fucked up this country.

"You need to come with us," a fat, ugly, bearded guy said.

"I don't think so," Babak responded

The other man, bearded with a rosary, ordered Babak to get into the vehicle.

"If you know what is best for you, get in the car."

Babak was aware of what could happen if he went with them.

"It is best for me not to get in the vehicle, and it is best for you to leave me alone," he said.

Babak knew that his only option was to fight them off.

One of the men grabbed his hand. Babak kicked him in the groin. In no time, Babak took both men down to the ground and kicked the shit out of them. He continued walking, knowing more of these guys would be coming after him soon, and he knew there was nothing he could do about that. He thought perhaps he should call his tough brother David. But he did not listen to his brother. He decided it was best to keep his brother out of this. David has a wife and two children to care for, and he also looks after their parents.

A black SUV stopped as he was crossing the street. Four men in dark clothing got out, all holding batons. They walked towards Babak. The first man to approach was an ugly, husky, and mean-looking man.

Babak thought he must kill that ugly bastard, and what happened after that, he did not give a shit.

When the man got close, Babak kicked him hard in the balls. The man cupped his nuts and fell. The other three were on him with their batons. Babak put up a good fight. They finally got him down. He tried to get on his feet, but they kept kicking and hitting him with batons. He curled into a ball on the sidewalk. The guy with a bloody nose continued kicking Babak.

"Enough. We are not supposed to kill the bastard; just give him the message," one of the guys said.

Chapter 24

The Message

It was dark at the end of the alley. The same SUV stopped, and two men got out. They lifted the back hatch and pulled Babak out. They hauled him to Babak's family's front door and dropped him on the concrete sidewalk. They rang the bell and left.

David opened the door and stared down at the bloodied Babak sitting against the wall.

"God damn you, Babak, I told you not to go into that fucking house. I had a bad feeling about that; I tried to warn you. Now, I must go to Sherin's house and kill all those fucking bastards." David said with much anger. He punched the brick wall.

"What the fuck, David? You should not have done that. I'll be okay. They had no involvement in this. It was their father's order," Babak said with a grunt.

***

Meanwhile, at Sherin's house.

Rafee was sitting in her wheelchair, wearing her pajamas. Farah was combing her mother's hair. Sherin stood by the window, holding her phone and lost in thought, gazing out at the studio, remembering the taste of his kiss on her lips. She tried not to cry over everything that had happened in her life. She thought about her mother and her younger brother, who disappeared, and how the family didn't know where they were or had graves to visit or mourn at. When she thought about losing and burying her daughter, her jaw clenched. A tear rolled down her face. She wiped her tears with her hand. Her heart ached deeply again. Rafee watched her.

"I like him, Mother. Tell me what kind of sin I have committed to deserve this pain. Is more coming? I am tired. I can't endure this. How did you survive, my poor dear mother? Why doesn't Father tell us where Mother and my brother are buried?

Everyone in the room teared up.

Rafee rolled her wheelchair to Sherin, held her hand, and kissed it.

"I survived, my dear, maybe because I love my children so much. I do not understand why he doesn't tell us," Rafee said.

"Mother, is he my father? You said you would tell me when I was older and more mature. Now is the time for you to tell me," Farah begs her mother.

"Please promise me that you will not hate Babak and me," Rafee said to her daughter.

"I could never hate you, mother. But he can go to hell," Farah said with hatred for Babak.

Rafee shook her head and stared at the floor.

She recalled the days with Farah's father, Babak.

"Yes," her mother whispered, as she continued to stare at the floor.

Chapter 25

Die to Love

It was the 1980s, just a few years after the Islamic Government occupied beautiful Iran and its rich and ancient culture, only to destroy it.

The young and beautiful Rafeegheh, in her mid-twenties, now wore a long-sleeved dress, a Montour, and a scarf around her head. The only skin visible was her face and hands. She stood by a steel door at a large, old two-story brick house, and nervously rang the bell. Leaning against the wall, she waited. Her heart pounded a mile a minute, and her mind was filled with worry and fear about what Babak might say, fearing that her heart might break again.

The door opened, and Babak, in his late twenties, stepped out, stood, and looked at her, frozen and shocked. Rafeegheh stood with her arms folded across her chest, her big, frightened eyes fixed on him. Without saying a word, he slowly walked toward her, took her hand, and gazed into her frightened and sad face.

His eyes teared up, and he felt like bawling, for some reason. After all, he had broken her heart.

They embraced and held each other.

"What a surprise, Rafeegheh, let's go in," Babak whispered.

"Babak, I would like us to go somewhere else if it is okay," she said nervously.

She had dreamed, thought, and planned about this moment if ever it came through.

They parted and looked at each other.

"Okay, let me change and tell my family that I am leaving," Babak told her.

Babak walked to the door, turned, looked at her, and entered the house

She smiled, and her heart calmed down while she waited.

***

She drove on the crowded streets of Tehran with Babak sitting in the passenger seat. They talked about today's events and the good old days. Finally, after a hectic drive, they arrived at her condo.

Babak stood in the middle of her moderately furnished and immaculate condo. He noticed and walked towards the paintings that hung on her walls. A seascape painting, a portrait painting of Rafeegheh, and more paintings by Babak decked the walls.

"This is a delightful place, Rafeegheh. I see you still have my paintings."

"Yes, remember you gave them to me before you left me and went to America," Rafeegheh told him from another room.

"Yes, I remember," said solemnly.

"I will keep and treasure them for the rest of my life. You know what, Babak? I was so scared to come to your house today, but I had to. I didn't know when I would see you again. I overheard that you were back visiting."

Classical music played in the background.

She walked into the room where Babak was waiting. She had changed into a blouse and a short skirt (the same clothes she had worn when they met before he left for America). Her beautiful, stylish short hair was exposed. She was holding two glasses of red wine. She handed one to him.

She looked like an actor from an old American movie.

"I remember those clothes. You are beautiful."

She smiled and nodded. "I was afraid you may not want to talk to me or see me, for that matter. You have no idea how happy I am," she said.

"How could you say that? I have missed you; you were and are a very special person to me."

160

"You never contacted me. I always asked about you, but everyone avoided sharing information about you, especially your sister, Mehri," Rafeegheh said. "I thought she liked me at one time."

"I often thought of you, in fact, very often, but I was unsure if seeing you would affect me. Besides, I was married," Babak told her.

"I understand your situation. I must say, you still are a woman killer. You should know you can't take a chance and go out after drinking this wine. If you get caught, you will get two hundred lashes in public, and if we sleep together and they find out, we both will be stoned to death in public," She explains and stares at him.

"It would be very romantic if we were both stoned together at the same time, something for the public to be entertained by and enjoy," he said.

You know, I am serious. Things have changed here. We were lucky that we did not get stopped and questioned about whether we were married or not. You are right, many people would love that," she said. Rafeegheh looked at him. She placed her hands on her heart and took a deep breath. They sat on the sofa and finished the rest of the wine with some pistachios, conversation, flirtation, and laughter. "I have dreamed and waited for this moment for so long. "You know what, Babak?" she asked him

"What Rafeegheh?"

"We owe it to each other," she said.

"Owe what?"

"The love we never made… And don't tell me that you never wanted me. I even wrote on the back of one of the pictures of you and me together that you could have me anytime you wanted." She said it with much desire on her face and in her words.

"I did want you, and I still have that picture. I always had enthusiastic respect for you. I would have slept with you if only we were engaged. You were too good for me, Rafeegheh."

"But I loved you, and I wanted you to make love to me before you left me. I did not care about the consequences. You have the picture, ha?" she asked.

"Yes, I hide it in my studio. My wife is a very jealous woman."

"I do not blame her," she said.

After finishing the rest of her wine, she got up and took his hand.

"Come with me. Please, do not say one word; you have made me wait and suffer enough." Her heart pounded frantically against her ribcage. He was torn between his marriage and her love for him, as well as his own love for her. He thought of the big argument his wife, Sarah, and he had had before he left America.

This was not lust; he was sure about this... This was love, a love like Romeo and Juliet, a love with an unhappy ending. Is it sympathy for her or to prove his genuine love for her and, most of all, himself? He knew that he would always love her.

She led him to the bathroom. He kisses her more tenderly and passionately than he has ever kissed anyone. She puts her fingers into his hair. He unbuttons her blouse as they kiss; she looks at him and tears up. He kisses her eyes, then moves his lips to her neck, then her chest, and finally to her beautiful breast that he had never seen or kissed before. He gets on his knees and kisses her stomach. He removes her skirt, and she shivers. He stands up and helps her to get undressed. She turns on the water. He notices the scars on her back; he kisses the wounds and gently touches them.

He said nothing, tears filling his eyes; she turned and embraced him.

"After you left for America, a few of my friends and I were arrested. They did much more horrible things to my

162

friend," she said with a shake of her head. "Awful things, Babak."

They step into the shower.

"I had never seen you completely naked; you have such a beautiful body."

She smiled and walked to him. After they kissed more, he held her up in his arms and made the most gentle and sweet love to her.

She had been saving herself just for him for all these years. She moaned and moaned, looked at him, and wept with a sweet smile as she climaxed.

They were both wrapped in a towel. He picked her up in his arms.

"Which way?" he asked.

She smiled, pointed, and wrapped her arms around his neck. They kissed as he carried her, and he gently laid her on the bed. Their bodies were now clean, and he deeply enjoyed touching her. His caresses profoundly moved her. He was exhilarated by making love to her, pouring out the most tender and sweet affection he had ever shared. He had never felt this way with any woman, not even with Roya or his wife, Sarah. Her heart pounded in her chest. He lay on his back while they held hands. He got up, went to the kitchen, and returned with two glasses of water. She sat beside him, and they drank some water, then placed their glasses on the nightstand.

"Come on top and be gentle," she asked."

They made love once more. She lay on top and kept kissing him.

"I love you," she grunt. "Now you know I haven't been with anyone else, nor have I wanted to. I knew one day I would see you and make you love me. I wanted you to be my first and last. Maybe twenty years from now, we'll run into each other and do this again."

He kissed her hand.

"Stay with me this evening, please," she asked.

***

The morning sun shone through the lace curtain onto the two of them. Rafeegheh rested her face on Babak's chest. She kissed it and ran her fingers through the hair on his chest. "I love you so much, Babak, even more now than ever; I feel complete. I wish I could die in your arms. My only wish is to DIE IN YOUR ARMS." He kissed her head.

"Do you know what, Rafeegheh?"

"What?" she asked in a whisper.

"I always loved you, but I loved you in a special way," Babak whispered.

"I know. Let's make breakfast, you and I, and eat together like happily married couples."

***

Now, let's go back to Sherin's house.

Farah stared at her mother.

"My dear Farah, he has never been told about you. I gave a letter to his sister and begged her to send it to him, but she never did. I want you to know that I needed part of him in my life to carry on, and you are that part. He is a good human being. Please do not hate him," Rafee begged.

Farah hugged her mother with tears in her eyes.

"Oh, my poor, dear mother. You should not have kept this secret for all these years. I am glad you finally lifted this weight off your heart. You are a true lover, mother."

Rafee looked at Sherin, who stood by the window, her arms crossed on her chest, holding her phone. She looked out into the moonlit garden and at her studio. She had not felt this happy for a long time, perhaps since the sweet days of her childhood with her mother.

Farah and Mehri sat on the sofa, looking at their phones. Ray played his violin. The phone on the wall rang, and Mehri answered it. She listened.

164

"Okay, thanks," she responded, then hung up the phone and looked at Rafee.

"He did not find Mr. Babak. Or perhaps he is hiding something," Mehri told Rafee.

"Okay, thank you, Mehri," Rafee said with disappointment.

Sherin gazed out the window, thinking about what the ten-year-old flower vendor had told Babak and her. "Your husband is nice. I hope you live together for a long time " Rafee interrupted Sherin's thoughts.

"Dear Sherin, he is probably home with his family. Try not to worry so," Rafee said.

Sherin nodded as she looked out. She felt nothing; she was numb.

"It has been almost three hours, Mother, and still no word from him," she whispered with a sigh. She leaned against the wall as her knees weakened, and she could hardly hold her weight. She felt like having a good cry again.

"He is probably embarrassed to call. We will call him tomorrow," Mehri told Sherin.

Sherin nodded. Ray stopped playing his violin, and the room was quiet for a few minutes.

The doorbell rang. Mehri went to the intercom and pressed the button.

"Who is it?" Mehri asked.

"It is David, Babak's brother. Open the fucking door."

Mehri looked at Rafee, and Rafee nodded yes.

"Okay, Mr. David. I will unlock the gate for you. Please come in,"

Mehri and Sherin waited outside on the lit porch as David approached, helping the injured Babak walk.

"Miss Sherin, this is all your fault. I warned him about your evil family, but he wouldn't listen. I brought him here so you can see what your fucking people have done to my brother."

165

"Mr. David, they are not our people; we hate them as much as you do. We had nothing to do with this. Please, let me take him to the hospital," Sherin said, frightened.

Sherin looked at Babak. His face was caked with blood.

"I will be fine. It was a message from your father. They told me to stay away from you and your house. I think it was the guard. When I was leaving, he called someone," Babak said, rubbing his side.

"Please come in and have some tea, Mr. David. I am sorry for what happened. We should tend to his wounds," Sherin said.

"No thanks. I will stay here," David said.

Sherin helped Babak inside as Farah stood in the foyer watching.

"Tell me what happened," Sherin asks Babak in a whisper.

"Why can't Father leave us alone? I will talk to him again and insist that he stays out of our lives, or kill all of us," Mehri told Sherin.

Babak looked at Sherin and whispered. "They wanted me to stay away from you."

"Did you fight them off for Sherin?" Mehri asked with a smile.

"It was crazy. What was I thinking? Look at me; they could have killed me," Babak said with a smirk; he joked with all the pain he had all over his body.

They went to the kitchen. Sherin hovered over Babak, who sat in a chair. His face and neck were cleaned up, and there was a bruise on his cheek. There were also some blood stains on his shirt.

"Thanks, Miss Sherin," he said.

Farah stepped into the kitchen. She looked remorseful.

"Mr. Babak. I am sorry," she said.

"It is okay. Come here, please," Babak asked Farah.

Farah walked over to him, and Babak took her hand in his.

"I would have done the same thing. I'm sorry, Farah; I was never told about you. When I first saw you, my heart trembled. You reminded me of your mother; you looked just like her when she was your age."

"Just tonight, Mother told me a little about you," Farah said.

Rafee entered the room in her wheelchair.

"Sherin is our private nurse. She does a decent job," Rafee told Babak. Rafee looked at Farah. "She's got your eyes and your spirit," Rafee told Babak. Babak searched for the resemblance in Farah's face.

"I am sorry," Babak told Rafee.

Rafee moved next to Babak. Sherin and Mehri left the room.

"Sherin was distraught and concerned about you. There is so much to talk about. She studied Biology and was researching DNA. She discovered something new about it and kept it to herself. Then, when that accident occurred, she dropped out of college and halted her research. She is a smart woman. Sherin and you need some time together so you can get to know each other a little better. Another thing I want you to do is to go to the supper club so you can see what this government is doing with our people's lives and money. Babak, I am happy for both of you. You must know she cares deeply for you," Rafee said.

"Yes, Father, I believe you and Sherin need that.

Babak nodded.

"I'll ask her to make a reservation. Well, I feel very exhausted. We can catch up later. Dear Farah, can you please get something for Babak and David to eat and drink?"

Chapter 26

Evin, the Most Infamous Prison

Sherin drove a red BMW with tinted windows through the busy streets of Tehran. Babak sat in the passenger seat. Sherin was entirely made up and dressed in fancy attire, including a scarf. Babak wore a suit and tie. They held hands and exchanged smiles.

"I hope you don't blame me for what they did to you. Mehri is going to give Father crap for his actions and involvement in that whole episode," Sherin told him.

"Of course, I don't blame you. I blame myself for standing up for you."

Sherin looked at him, smiled, and shook her head. She continued driving, keeping a close eye on the road. She glanced over at him and then looked back at the traffic.

"Now that you risked your life for me, I can trust you enough to tell you something. You can't tell anyone, including the children. Only Rafee and I know about this." She glanced at Babak. "We all have business visas to go to America. My father is a very wealthy and influential man. He fears things will change with this government. He said a few government workers are spying for Israelis and want us to leave the country, but Rafee intends to stay. She says that she is going to die soon and wishes to be buried on the skirt of the mountain near our house. We can't leave her behind. We don't care about the consequences."

"I promise I will keep your secret. But I must know what happened to Rafee? The once vibrant and energetic person has now become frail and is bound to a life in a wheelchair. I did not recognize her at all."

"I will tell you the whole story after dinner," she said.
She drove down a long, private drive lined with Trees and lights on both sides.

"I have only been here once with Ray to see what kind of place it was. I honestly thought I would never come back. I want to tell you something, Babak. My father was one of the men involved in the arson of the cinema Rex, which resulted in the killing of over six hundred innocent people. The Islamic regime blamed it on the Shah, and the gullible people believed that," she told him.

"I, who loved the Pahlavi, also believed in all those lies that the Mullahs told us in the mosque. I feel very ashamed of that."

Sherin stopped the car in front of a large brick building. Two uniformed men approached the vehicle and opened the doors for Sherin and Babak. Sherin and Babak sat across from each other at a table laden with colorful food, including the finest caviar in the world. Babak inspected his surroundings. Women were dressed in expensive clothing, dripping with diamonds and gold, their scarves covering only half of their heads. Men were bearded and wearing suits. A young woman smiled at Babak. Sherin kicked him under the table.

"I didn't smile back," he leaned over and whispered.

"Good, I am watching," she whispered with a smile.

"Do not look. The man in a white suit, with the beautiful young lady, a couple of tables behind me, is her pimp and big drug dealer. She is going to end up in Dubai someday. All these men and women are part of the government mafia and cartels, and they have their hands in drugs, money laundering, and human trafficking. Most of them know my father. My father is as crooked as they are. The card I showed the people at the door can almost get me anywhere."

"Your look could almost get you anywhere or anyone," Babak said.

She gives him a flirty look and a smile.

Babak smiled, then looked around at the room's richness.

"What you see here are the riches imported from Europe," Sherin whispered.

Babak and Sherin just nibbled on the food, deep in thought. Finally, they left the supper club.

Babak and Sherin sat in her car on a hilltop beside a quiet road with big mansions around them. Kissing and gazing out over the lit-up city of Tehran. American oldies played on the car speakers.

"Aren't you concerned if the police stop here?" he asked.

"No one is going to bother us here. This is the government's rich kids' playground. Besides, I have my card."

"Would you go on a trip for a few days with me?" he asked.

"Yes, I would, but where? We can't get a hotel room. We aren't married," she responded.

"We can use your card or get one of those Islamic temporary marriage licenses for a small fee," Babak said and smiled.

"Okay. If you promise to tell me about this, Roya, who broke your heart and made you leave Iran. Rafee mentioned your tenant, Roya, but I never heard the full story. She said she saw you two holding hands and kissing in a movie theater, and then Rafee quickly left the theater. Also, Rafee said that Roya was much older but a beautiful woman. I don't know why Rafee never mentioned your name. She always referred to you as her dear friend," Sheerin concluded.

"I never told Rafee anything about Roya. I was unaware that she had seen us."

After a moment, Babak inquired, "Sherin, please tell me what happened to Rafee. I blame myself, and I should burn in hell for hurting such an angel."

"No, Babak, don't think or say such a thing. It must have been a tough decision to make; you were only in your twenties; what do we know when we are that young? Now, I know you truly loved and cared for Rafee," Sherin said.

"I will never forget Rafee weeping and begging me to take her to America."

After a few minutes of silence, Sherin began her story.

"Rafee lived with us after her own family cast her out because of her love child, Farah. Well, you and her child. The day she was arrested, Farah was just four years old. This was before the mass executions of thousands of political prisoners and many innocent protesters, all carried out by these so-called religious people. It began on July 19, 1998, and lasted for several months. This is what my blessed Mother told me. It was an extremely challenging time for people in Iran. The inflation, the harsh rules, arresting and torturing and hanging people, and stoning women in public were standard practices by the government in those days. Right after the damn revolution, all the prisoners were released, and most of them were murderers, thieves, and rapists who joined the government in different sectors. They would easily kill anyone at the order of the upper hand so heartlessly. Most of them were given guns, and these people killed so many innocents on the streets."

"This was the day of what happened to Rafee and Farah."
***

Thousands of protesters once again crowded the streets of Tehran, Iran.

"Free the prisoners. Freedom of vote. These were the repeated chants on the streets of Tehran, as well as in many cities across Iran."

Rafee, in her twenties, dressed according to Islamic laws, and her daughter, Farah, four, stood on the second-floor balcony of a two-story brick home. They watched the crowd on the streets.

"Mommy, can we please go outside?" Farah begged her mother.

"Honey, it is not safe to be out there," Rafee said as she touched Farah's hair.

"But Mommy, look at all those kids." Farah pointed out.

"But they are taking a risk, honey," Rafee said.

"Please, Mommy? I want to take a risk, too."

"Honey, do you even know what risk is?"

"No," Farah responded.

"Do you know why we have this railing here?" Rafee asked.

"Yes, so we won't fall."

"Right. Would you walk on this railing?" Rafee asked.

"No, Mommy, that is dangerous," Farah answered.

"Honey, taking a risk means doing something that could be dangerous."

"But, Mommy, we're going to walk on the street, not the railing."

Farah kissed Rafee's hand and gave a begging look.

"Let's go inside and ask Aunt Maheen and see what she says," Rafee said.

They went to the kitchen. Farah walked over and hugged Maheen's legs as she was preparing a meal. Rafee watched anxiously.

"Aunt Maheen, please, please say yes. Can Mommy and I go outside?"

Maheen smiled and wiped her hands with a towel. Maheen pinched Farah's cheek lightly.

"Okay, dear, yes, you can," she said, but not wholeheartedly.

"Freedom to vote! Free the prisoners." In Maheen's kitchen, we heard the demonstrators chant this slogan repeatedly.

"Please, my dear Rafee, be very careful and stay close to home. You know what will happen once you are arrested. Supper will be ready very soon, and Sherin and Mehri will be home for dinner. But Ray and Samon will not join us; they will stay with their father tonight," Maheen told Rafee.

"We will be very careful," Rafee told Maheen.

"Death to the dictator, free the prisoners," chanting echoed on the streets of Tehran. The Revolutionary Guards were everywhere, and Mozdours and Besiegees walked amongst the protesters, disguised as ordinary people. Many Revolutionary Guards, armed with their guns, were strategically placed on the rooftops.

Suddenly, tear gas was thrown out at the demonstrators, and the peaceful demonstration turned into a riot. Injured victims fell to the ground. The Revolutionary Guard and the militants arrested the young and the old.

Rafee held Farah tightly in her arms, trapped in havoc. Two Mozdours grabbed her by the arms as she struggled to get away.

"You must come with us," they ordered as they held her.

Rafee was terrified and wept.

"We did not do or say anything, I swear. Please, our home is just half a block away. Please let us go home. At least let me take my child home. Please?" Rafee begged in tears.

They dragged Rafee as she held Farah, who was crying.
***

Rafee shook, holding Farah tight in her arms. She was herded by two prison guards through the bright, long, and damp hallway with blood stains on the concrete floor. Sounds of crying and screams filled the air. Farah was frightened.
***

"Evin Prison, in Tehran, Iran, is the most infamous prison. It is known as Evin University due to the number of students who are imprisoned there. Torture, rapes, and beatings take place here daily, no matter their age, sex, or innocence."

***

Rafee stood with Farah in her arms before a husky and bearded interrogator, who sat behind a desk with a rosary in his hand. A torturer and a rapist stood at his side.

"Let's go home, Mommy. I'm scared to be here. Aunt Maheen said supper would be ready soon," Farah told her mother.

The torturer stepped forward, grabbed the child's face, and said
"Shut the fuck up, kid." Then he shook her head and pushed it back to Rafee's chest.

"Please be quiet," Rafee whispers to the frightened Farah.

"Sit in that chair," the interrogator ordered Rafee. Rafee sat and held Farah in her arms. "Please, God, hear me now. If ever you are to prove your existence to me, please have mercy on my child and protect her here in this hell." Rafee, in silent prayer, begged God in her heart. Her prayer was not answered when she was imprisoned and tortured a few years ago in this same prison.

"So, you are not happy with the Islamic law and want to change it? Why don't you people respect and obey our mighty leader and be satisfied with what you have?" The interrogator said. Then he slammed his hand down on the desk where he sat.

Farah jumped and cried.

"I want to go home Mommy," Farah whispers to her mother.

"Shh," Rafee whispered. "We will go home soon. You must be quiet, please, honey," Rafee teared up, thinking about what they did to her and her friends in this same prison. The scars on her back and mind would never go away.

"Take the child from the whore and tie her down," the interrogator ordered the men.

The men forcefully pried the screaming Farah from her mother's arms and handcuffed Farah to an old cast-iron radiator using dirty old rags.

Rafee sat on an old wooden chair, handcuffed behind her back. Her feet were bound together by some rope.

The rapist stood behind Rafee. He touched her breast with one hand, fondling himself with the other. He kissed her neck and moaned. The other two men watch with a devilish smile.

"She has nice, firm tits. I am ready to fuck her now," The rapist told the interrogator.

"You had enough for now. Go stand next to him," the interrogator said.

"Tell me, what organizations do you belong to? And give me all their names," the interrogator asked Rafee, then got up and walked towards her, thumbing his rosary.

"I swear, sir —"

"Shut up, you stupid, lying whore," The interrogator told her.

"Tie her to the bed," he orders the men.

Rafee lay gagged face down on an old wooden bed. Her hands and bare feet were bound with ropes, securing her to the bedposts with a blanket on her back. Her back and feet were wiped with a tractor alternator belt. Through her half-open, tearful eyes, she saw her frightened daughter, Farah, shaking as she was restrained alone in the corner, watching all of this in terror. This sight would haunt Farah for the rest of her life.

***

The blanket was used as a barrier that prevented the tractor belt from tearing the skin, but it left large blisters instead. On the following day, the men would remove the victim's clothing and beat them with a car alternator belt that tore into their skin, causing small chunks of flesh to fly in the air and leave deep, open wounds.

***

The door opened. A prison guard dragged a young girl in; she was in her late teens.

"Please, sir, let me go home! I swear I am innocent," she told the interrogator.

"She is wild and feisty, Hagee," the prison guard informed the interrogator. They took Rafee and tied her to the radiator next to Farah. The young girl was secured to a chair facing Rafee and Farah. The interrogator stood before the young girl, staring at her large breasts.

"If you sit quietly and obey, I will send you home tonight. By now, I am sure your parents are very worried about you, right?" he asked her.

"Yes, sir, especially my sick mother."

The interrogator walks behind the girl.

"Have you finished high school yet?" he asked the teen.

"No, sir. I am only in tenth grade," she turned her head and told him.

"But you look so grown up," he said with lust in his voice.

He gently touched her face and ran his finger across her lips. As he did so, he looked over at Rafee and slowly moved his hand to the young girl's breasts.

The young girl startled.

"What are you doing, sir? Please don't touch me there. Please. Don't you have a daughter?" she asked him with a stern tone.

"Do not speak if you want to go home tonight. Do you want to be kept here for years, with a different guard visiting you each night?" the interrogator asked her.

176

She looks at Rafee. Rafee bit her lip and shook her head. Please, God, have mercy on her. Who are these evils? What has happened to humanity? Rafee thought.

The young girl trembled as the interrogator unbuttoned her blouse and slid his hand under her bra. Rafee turned her head away.

"I want you to watch me whore, you are next," the interrogator said.

Rafee reluctantly looked as he pulled the girl's bra up, exposing her breasts. The two other men moaned at the sight.

"What the hell are you doing, sir? I am a virgin, you stupid man. Don't you have a daughter?" the teen told him with a stern tone.

The men laughed.

"Why does nobody listen to me?" he said

He stepped back and suddenly kicked the teen with his army boot in the knee, toppling her chair over. He watched her gasp for air. Her knee split open and bled. Rafee closes her eyes, tears rolling down her face.

"So, you are a virgin? I will be your cherry picker today, honey."

Men laughed. The young girl cried.

"Sir, I am sorry. I beg you, please let me go home," she apologized hopelessly.

The two other men unfastened her hands from the chair, dragged her to the wooden bed, and placed her on her back with her blouse, skirt, and underclothes removed. They fastened the frightened girl's hands and feet to the bedposts while her knees bled and she cried.

"You two can go out now," the interrogator told the guys.

"Okay, Hagee. Have fun," one of the men said.

"How many times do I have to tell you, stupid guys? We do not do this to the virgins to have fun; we do it so that after they die, they go to hell, not to heaven."

"Sorry, Hagee," the man apologized, and they left the cell room.

The Interrogator stood over the girl. He bent over and touched her breasts. She looked over to Rafee, her eyes pleading.

"I want you to watch me; you are the next whore," he told Rafee as Farah hid behind her mother.

Rafee watched helplessly as the interrogator unzipped his pants and climbed on top of her, then savagely raped the crying young girl as she cried out in pain. Then he left the cell room.

Rafee looked at a gold-threaded wall hanging.

It read "Allahu Akbar." GOD IS MERCIFUL.

"Is this the true faith of this religion?" Rafee thought.

The young girl lay on the wooden bed, silently weeping.

"Is it over? Is he done with me? Is he going to let me go home now? Oh God, I hope I die here; I can never face my family," she told Rafee as she wept.

Rafee wept. The terrified Farah looked at her mother and burst into tears.

"The interrogator has visited Mecca at least once to purify himself from evil thoughts and actions. In undertaking such travel, he was awarded the title "Hagee."

The door opened, and the interrogator, torturer, and rapist entered.

"Can I go home now, please? Sir, please?" The teen begged the interrogator.

"What is the hurry?' the rapist told the teen and looked at Rafee.

"You are next, whore," he said.

The men approach the young girl. Each man took turns raping her. She grew unconscious from the continuous abuse.

Hagee sat at his desk, watching and thumbing his rosary.

***

Rafee, Farah, and the young girl slept on the concrete floor of the bright cell room.

They were startled awake by the noise of the heavy steel door as two guards entered the cell with a bag of salt. They kicked Rafee and the teen's blistered feet, and they dumped the salt onto their bloody and broken wounds. The women screamed. Farah shivered.

"Get up, both of you," Guard #1 orders Rafee and her daughter.

"Get up whore," Guard #2 kicked the teen.

"I can't. My knee is broken, and the blood and the skin have dried on the floor," she said through her tears.

Guard #2 grabbed her arm and pulled her up. She screamed as the skin around her knee tore open and bled.

***

Rafee sat with her daughter against the wall in the bright hallway. About a half dozen women, young and old, sat on the concrete floor, their hands bound behind them, and their wounded and bloody feet were starched and bound.

Farah sat beside her mother, terrified. Across from them sat a fourteen-year-old girl with a badly bruised face and raw wounds on her feet. She looked at Farah and offered a smile. Then she starts weeping.

"Yesterday was my fourteenth birthday --- I was raped last night by two men. They tore my vagina," she told Rafee with a painful laugh. Then she burst into tears, and the women wept.

"I am so sorry, my dear, so sorry," Rafee said with a big lump in her throat and tears in her eyes.

"We are so sorry," the group of women told her.

Rafee turned and watched as four uniformed, masked men approached the prisoners. They kicked at the prisoners' inflamed feet. One woman in her fifties, fainted from the pain. One of the men moved toward the fourteen-year-old. The hall was filled with terrified screams.

Rafee scooted forward and dropped herself toward the man's feet.

"Please, Sir. Just look at her. She is only a young child and already in so much pain. I beg you, sir," Rafee begged in tears.

Suddenly, another man kicked Rafee hard in her lower back. Rafee fell on the concrete floor in excruciating pain, and she gasped for air.

"If any of you stick your nose in our business, this is what is going to happen to you bitches," said the masked man with an Arabic accent.

   ***

Babak and Sherin sat in her car with emotions flowing. Babak had his arms crossed on his chest. He looked out at the city lights.

"With my father's orders, three days later, Rafee and Farah were released from prison, and my blessed mother took them to the hospital. It was then that we learned that Rafee would be paralyzed for the rest of her life. We also found out that she had a weak heart. The doctors told my mother that there was nothing they could do for her heart, except medicine that she would have to take for the rest of her life. They were uncertain of how long she would live. Shortly after that, my mother was killed, and Rafee raised us."

Sherin said and looked at him as he stared out.

"I am deeply sorry, Babak," she said, touching his hand.

Babak slightly shook his head.

There was a long silence.

180

"If I had taken her with me to America, this would not have happened to her," he said.

"Look at me, Babak. No one, not you or anyone else, knew what was going to happen to Iran and millions of innocent people. I want to tell you something, Babak."

He looked at her.

"You can't blame yourself for that. They do this to the prisoners all the time. Listen, I know you are a nice person. Rafee would not have loved you as she did. It moved me when you took Omeed to the soccer game, bought him a nice soccer ball, and took him out to eat. You have no idea how happy he was. He admires you."

She kisses his hand.

"Omeed lost his father to drugs. He never had a real father. I appreciate your kindness to him. I think of him as my little brother."

"He is such a sweet and polite boy. Seeing all those boys and girls picking up plastic bottles and scavenging for food from dumpsters breaks my heart. Thank you for tonight and for sharing with me about what happened to Rafee and Farah; what the two of them went through is horrific—poor Farah, my dear daughter."

Sherin drove through traffic holding Babak's hand.

Chapter 27

Price of Freedom

Babak, Ray, Mehri, David, and Moe are part of a crowd demonstrating and chanting on an overpass. The streets are overflowing with people and revolutionary guards, and Mozdours are everywhere.

Two Mozdours grab a young girl and lift her over their heads. The crowd watches in horror as they approach the guardrail and toss the screaming girl into the traffic below.

"Oh, my God! They threw my friend off the bridge, and no one came to aid her! What is wrong with you fucking people standing there recording with your damn phones?" a young lady cried out.

Mehri walked over to the lady and hugged her.

Protesters chanted, "Death to the dictator—death to the dictator."

Ray waved his cane in the air and chanted, gaining the attention of four Mozdours in civilian clothing.

"Death to the dictator - death to the government," Ray yelled.

The Mozdours grabbed him by the arms.

Mehri tried to stop the men.

One of the men hit Mehri on the head with his baton.

"Ouch! You son of a bitches." Mehri yelled.

She put one hand on her head while holding Ray's arm. Babak, David, and Moe confronted the men; the first one to approach with a baton, David threw a punch at the guy, knocking him back. They brought them to the ground and kicked the guys so they couldn't get up. The four of them ran off with Ray hobbling, on their way home.

***

Mehri and Babak stood in the family room. She removed her scarf.

"I hope you burn in hell, Ayatollah Khomeini. Burn in hell," Mehri said.

Babak examined her head. Sherin and Rafee entered the room. "What happened, honey?" Sherin asked.

"Those sons of bitches, hit me on the head with their baton," Mehri told her mother and her sister.

"The God damn Mozdours threw a girl off the bridge into the traffic below. It was such an awful scene, mother, so terrible. Then they tried to take Ray away, but... Moe, David, and Babak rescued Ray; they almost killed the damn Mozdours," Mehri added.

"Where are Ray, David, and Moe?" Rafee asked.

"They are outside smoking," Mehri answered.

"It is just a big bump. Put some ice on it. It will help the swelling go down," Babak told Mehri.

Moe, David, and Ray walked in.

"Miss Rafee, hello, I just came in to say goodbye," Moe said.

"I am glad you didn't leave. I wanted to say thank you," Mehri told Moe.

"It is okay, Mehri."

Moe hugged Babak and kissed him three times on the cheeks. Moe walked to Rafee and kissed her on the forehead.

"Take care of yourself, Rafee, my dear old friend," Moe said sincerely.

"It's always good to see you, Moe, and you as well, David," Rafee said.

"Babak, are you going home or staying here for a while longer?" David asks his brother.

"He is staying with your permission, Mr. David," Farah said.

"He has my permission. I will see you all later."

Moe and David left the room.

"Babak, would you please come to my room for a minute? After you are finished with Mehri," Rafee asked.

"She is okay, I will follow you," he said.

Babak sat on a chair next to Rafee's desk. Rafee was in her wheelchair behind the desk.

"We were so worried about all of you. I am glad you all made it back safely. When Farah speaks of you, she refers to you as a father, and I could also see her concern. I hope you stay for a while and spend time with her before you leave again for America. I don't know how long I will be around. Take the children with you to America. They all have visas and plenty of money. As long as I am alive, they will not go. They are trapped here because of me."

"Do not speak like that, Rafee. Kids love you. Everything will change soon. I am planning to stay a little longer. And I promise to take them with me when the time comes."

"Thank you. I was always so worried about my children. Now I know you will care for them; I will be at peace."

She took his hand to her lips and kissed it tenderly.

"You will always be in my heart," Rafee told him.

"And you will in mine, Rafee."

Chapter 28

Rafee's Only Wish

Everyone was gathered in the kitchen of Sherin's house. Drinks, snacks, and fancy glasses were arranged on the large kitchen table where Ray stood mixing drinks. They sat at the table talking and laughing.

"What would you like to drink tonight, Mr. Babak? Long Island tea, scotch, tequila, a martini?" Ray asked.

"Wow, a real bartender, and a real bar. I was not expecting this in Iran. How about a Long Island tea," Mr. Ray.

"You have no idea what is happening in people's homes here in Iran: alcohol, drugs, sex, and more," Ray updated Babak.

"That is why the number of people who have AIDS is so high in Iran, and there is not enough medicine," Farah said.

"So many people die from sickness, drug abuse, car accidents, and, of course, pollution," Rafee said.

"And alcohol. Well, Ray makes strong drinks," Sherin told Babak.

"Good, we all need a strong drink tonight. This is a very special night for me," Babak said.

"I will start with one of those, Ray," Rafee said.

"Oh my God! I don't think it is a good idea with all of your medications, Mother. Why don't you have a little wine?" Farah was overly concerned about her mother's health.

"Oh, honey, I have been waiting for this night for a long time. I don't give a damn about stupid medicine, and I am tired of this ridiculous wheelchair. I am ashamed of being such a burden to you all these years," she told Farah.

"But, mother," Farah said worriedly.

"My dear, please let me have my special night with all the people that I dearly love. I am waiting for my drink, sir," Rafee told Ray.

"One Long Island tea is coming up for our dear Mother Rafee. And we drink to our beloved mother and poor little brother's souls in heaven. We wouldn't have been here if it weren't for you, Mother," Ray told her, all choked up.

"I love all of you," Rafee told them.

"And we will drink to those who are in prison and the ones who have sacrificed their life for our country, to freedom," Babak said.

After everyone got their drink, they all cheered and drank.

Babak sat and looked at Rafee. He could understand her pain and suffering. He hoped that she would not do what he thought she might.

Sherin looks at Babak.

They drank, joked, and laughed out loud.

"Mother, I have never seen you laugh like this, ever," Farah told her mother and hugged her. Then, she returned to her chair.

"We all need another round, but none of that shit for me. How do people drink this? I want a double martini with four olives, please," Rafee told Ray.

"After that, Mother, you should quit. I think you need to take your medicine and call it a night," Farah told her mother.

"Yes, honey," Rafee responds, very drunk.

Rafee told everyone about the time that Babak was stuck in the chimney.

They all had a wonderful time drinking and laughing. Babak told them the funniest joke he knew. Sherin looked at Babak, laughing and shaking her head.

"You are so funny, Father, so amusing," Farah told him.

Please, God, do not take him away from me, Sherin prayed as she stared at her drink.

"I need a hug from everyone before I go to bed," Rafee told them.

They all went to her and hugged her.

"Babak, could you please help me find my room?" Rafee asks Babak.

He walked behind her wheelchair, pushing it.

Babak sat across from Rafee in her bedroom, and they held hands.

"Don't, Rafee. Please," Babak asks her.

"I am tired, Babak, tired," she said.

There was a chilling silence.

They held hands, and he placed his forehead on hers.

"Maybe this was our fate. If we had gotten married, our love may have turned bitter," he whispers.

"Perhaps, Babak, I'm so happy we met again, and you know about our beautiful daughter. Good night, my dear. Please watch over my children."

"I will. Good night."

He kissed her on the cheeks and left the room. He did not know what to do. To him, that was Rafee's living wish.

Chapter 29

Is This Love?

Babak follows the tipsy Sherin up the stairs to the guest bedroom.

The tipsy Sherin shows where everything is in the guest bedroom. She opens the dresser drawer.

"There are more towels here, so you should be all set. I have never had so much to drink. You are a fun person to have a drink with, Mr. Babak."

She leaned against the dresser.

He nodded as she talked, and he looked upset.

"What is wrong, dear?" She asked softly.

"I am worried about Rafee. I hope she does not do anything to hurt herself."

"We always worry about her. She sometimes gets depressed and weeps, which concerns us, too, but tonight, she was so happy. Do not worry, okay?" she asked him and kissed him on the lips.

"Thank you. I had no idea how funny you could be. We all had a fun time. You are a fun person to have a drink with," she repeated so seductively that he could not help but kiss her, and she was longing to kiss him all night. She closed her eyes, and they kissed hard. He pulled back to look at her, and she smiled.

"What?" she asks.

"You have stirred a desire feeling in me and I can't fight it," Babak whispered.

He kissed her, holding the back of her neck with one hand, and placed the other on her side, slowly moving it to her breast. She moaned and pushed him onto the bed. They undressed under the sheets and threw their clothes on the floor. Sherin climbed on top of him, straddling him, and she breathed hard. Her hair was wild on her face and neck. He kissed her breast as she made love to him with her wildest climax. He waited a minute for her to catch her breath, and then he climbed on top. First, he looked at her lustfully, then he did what he is best at, making love. He made her moan and cuss. Finally, after a long grunt, he collapsed on her.

"I need water," she mumbled after she caught her breath.

He got out of bed and poured some water from the pitcher into a glass. As he was getting the water, she looked at his body and shook her head. When he turned, she blew him a kiss. He smiled and handed her the water. She sat up, took the glass, and started to drink. He bit her ear.

They lay holding each other under the sheet with half of their body exposed.

"I thought I was going to have a heart attack," she whispered. "I wish I could stay with you for the rest of the night, but I'd better go," she whispered.

"Yes," he whispered.

Sherin placed her face on his chest.

"Are you going to leave me?" she asked in a whisper.

"What do you mean?" he asked.

"You know, leave me, go away."

"Not willingly," he answered.

"What does that mean?" she asked.

"Unless I die," he whispered.

"I won't let that happen," she looked at him and kissed him.

She fell asleep on him. He smiled and kissed her on her head.

Later, she woke up lying beside him, her arm on his chest. She looked at the clock on the wall, kissed him, and smiled.

"It is five in the morning, I'd better go," she whispered.

He looked at her and touched her hair.

"Yes, you should," he whispered.

189

She kissed him and got out of bed. He watched her getting dressed, her back to him.

"I want you to sit for me so I can paint you in the nude. Maybe one day, your portrait will end up in a museum for the public to see and admire your beauty," he said.

"Maybe," she turned and smiled, sending him a kiss.

" Does that mean you are okay with that?" he asked.

"I will pose for you as you wish," she said, kissed him, and then left the room.

"She wore me out," he said, stretched his body, and closed his eyes.

190

Chapter 30

Love and Sacrifice

Babak prepared breakfast and set the table. Coffee was made. Sherin entered the kitchen. Babak looked at her. She kissed him.

"Good morning," she said.

"Good morning," he said.

"Are we okay?" he asked.

"Yes," she whispered and nodded.

She grabbed a coffee cup and poured some coffee.

Ray hobbled in with his cane.

"Good morning. Smells good. What are you making, Mr. Babak?" he asked.

"Good morning, Mr. Ray. French toast with your good French bread," Babak responded.

"Ah. You made coffee. Good morning, Sherin," Ray said.

"Good morning, Ray."

Ray poured a cup, walked towards the porch, and left the kitchen.

Sherin took a bite of French toast.

"This is delicious, Mr. Babak."

"Thanks."

Farah entered the kitchen with her hand on her forehead.

"Oh God, I have such a nasty headache," Farah complained.

"Good morning, dear. I'm sorry. I think we all had too much to drink. Have some coffee; it might help," Babak said with much concern.

"I will, Father. Good morning, Sherin. Is breakfast ready?" Farah asked.

"Yes, dear, I am almost finished," he answered.

He walked over to his daughter and kissed her forehead.

"I am sorry, dear, would you mind waking Mehri and Mother, please?" he asked his daughter.

"Okay, Father," she said.

Babak hugged her. Sherin looked at him and nodded.

"I am sorry about your headache. Do you have some medicine for that?"

Farah placed her arms around him and whispered, "Yes."

"I should go and wake them up," she said.

***

Farah stood outside her mother's bedroom door and knocked once.

"Mother, it is time to rise and shine," she said.

Farah knocked again. Her hand was on her forehead, and her face was filled with excruciating pain.

"My alcoholic mother, good morning, are you up?"

She knocked again.

" Father has made a good breakfast. Are you joining us?"

Farah gently pushed the door open. Rafee was sitting in her wheelchair, facing the window. Mountains were seen in the distance. Her head was down.

"Good morning, mother."

There was no answer. Farah walked over, put her hands on her mother's shoulder, bent, and kissed her head.

"That was too much drinking, mother."

Rafee mumbles something. Farah notices a photo of her mother and Babak on her lap.

"What did you say, Mother? Farah walked around to face Rafee,"

"Get your father," Rafee grunted.

Farah looked at her Rafee's breath was labored. Farah ran to the door and called out.

"Father, please come. Come quickly," Farah shouted.

Babak ran. Sherin followed. They entered the room, and he looked to see what was wrong with Rafee. He asked Farah and Sherin to help get Rafee off the wheelchair and into his arms as he sat on the floor.

"Farah, please go and get everyone," he said to his daughter.

Babak held Rafee in his arms. Rafee's breath was rugged and raddled.

"What is wrong, Babak?" Sherin asked.

"I am sorry, she is going to leave us, Sherin."

The children gathered in the room.

"Should we call the doctor?" Ray asked Babak, worried.

Babak looked at him with teary eyes. Shook his head no.

"I'm sorry, it's too late. Last night she said goodbye to me."

Everyone looked at Babak.

Babak was emotional.

"Rafeegheh, all your children are here—our beautiful daughter, Farah, Sherin, Mehri, and Ray," Babak said, choked and emotional.

Rafee could hardly breathe. Her eyes were fixed on Babak. Everyone wept, and Babak talked to her as he choked.

"Do you remember? On our visit twenty-one years ago, it was morning, just like today, and you were in my arms just like now. Remember, you smiled and said that you wished to..."

Babak stops and wipes his tears away with his hand. With a lump in his throat, he said, "Die in your arms." You are now in your Babak's arms.

She smiled a little. A tear rolled from the corner of her eye down onto her face. He wiped it with his hand. She nodded, looked at everyone, softly squeezed Babak's hand, and took her last breath with his hand in hers and with a beautiful smile.

There will be a stain of guilt in Babak's heart until he takes his last breath, for not taking Rafee to America with him when she begged. He left Iran and her behind.

***

Babak and Rafeegheh, both in their twenties, hiked up a snowy mountainside in Tehran, Iran. Rafeegheh scooped a handful of fresh snow and packed it into a snowball. Babak walked ahead of her and was surprised when a neck full of fluffy, cold, wet snow hit him. He turned around, and she laughed as she ran backward until she disappeared into the snowy mist.

Epilogue
Good Life in America

Babak honored his promise to Rafeegheh. He arranged everything and took the children to America.

Farah and Mehri sat with their hair styled and exposed. Ray sat between them, and they all slept on a crowded airplane. Farah woke up as she sat on the aisle seat across from her father. Babak looked at her and then reached for her hand. They held hands. Sherin sat next to Babak by the window. They held hands. Her uncovered head rested on Babak's shoulder. She looked at him, and they kissed.

"We are going to have a good life together in America," Babak whispers to Sherin.

"I'm worried," she whispered.

"There's no reason to worry. You can continue your research."

She gazed out the window at the scene far below.

"Is that the Statue of Liberty?" she asked Babak.

"Yes. Dear Farah, look outside and wake Mehri and Ray so they can see.

My heart goes out to all the people who are suffering in Iran. Approximately eight percent of the population lives in poverty in a country that is rich in culture and resources.

Women Life Freedom

Evin Prison

Under current Islamic law in Iran, an individual is considered criminal and guilty of slander if they engage in any form of speech that questions the religion and its regime. This individual is deemed guilty without trial or defense; questions go unasked. Evin Prison is sometimes referred to as Evin University due to the large number of students who are imprisoned there. It stands as the world's most brutal and infamous prison. Beatings, torture, rape, mock executions, and brutal interrogations are the norm at Evin, where for the last three decades the anguished cries of prisoners have been swallowed by the drab walls of the low-slung lockup in northwestern Tehran. Nestled at the foot of the Alborz Mountains, it is home to an estimated 15,000 inmates, including killers, thieves, and rapists.

Victims have reported that this kind of punishment is one of the most painful experiences a person can endure. No one could have imagined how painful this was, thinking the blanket would be a barrier to protect the skin. A person would develop a large blister on their back and the bottoms of their feet from a large belt. The next day or two, they would then take these same innocent people and beat them again using a narrower alternator belt. This would rip through their clothing and tear into their skin, causing it to fly into the air.

Novels in Progress

Viola Wore Sorrow Like Satin
"The Bitter Pour"
A novel by Naser D. Shahrivar
Set in the early 1900s, Viola Wore Sorrow Like Satin /
The Bitter Pour, tells the heartfelt story of a German
immigrant family who settles in the riverside town of
Guttenberg, Iowa. With dreams of starting a new life, they
buy an old brewery and begin making beer based on tradition
and pride. But when the mother (Esther) dies suddenly, their
strict Aunt Anna arrives from the old country to take control,
enforcing strict rules that ban alcohol, music, and even
marriage.

Decades later, Viola Jungk, one of the daughters, now an
elderly woman living alone in the shadow of the shuttered
brewery, receives a visit from a curious young mother eager to
uncover the building's history. What starts as a simple
question turns into an unforgettable afternoon as Viola opens
a long-hidden bottle of wine and shares her family's turbulent
past – the pain of forbidden love, a tragic murder, and the
bitter betrayal that led to the brewery's violent closure by anti-
alcohol crusaders.

Through Viola's voice, the story explores the powerful
effect of words – how gossip, judgment, and deceit can
destroy lives and legacies Viola Wore Sorrow Like Silk / The
Bitter Pour is a haunting, deeply human story of love lost,
dreams stolen, and the resilience of the heart in the face of
injustice.

Rich in setting, Viola Wore Sorrow Like Silk / The Bitter Pour captures a crucial moment in American history while weaving a deeply personal story about control, betrayal, and silencing women's voices. Perfect for fans of Kristin Hannah, Kate Morton, and Lisa Wingate, this novel appeals to readers of historical fiction with emotional depth, family secrets, and social relevance.

The Call of Evil

The Call of Evil is a compelling story about two true lovers—Yasha, an emerging artist, and Sophia, a talented travel writer—whose lives are shattered by a single, horrifying act of evil.

The novel explores what drives people to commit such darkness. Evil is complex. It often stems from a mix of psychological, emotional, and social issues, such as a lack of empathy, the desire to dominate others, or deep insecurity masked by cruelty.

At a friend's birthday party, Sophia becomes the victim of a brutal assault by two men, an act so devastating that it leads her to take her own life. Her death sends Yasha into a spiral of grief and hopelessness. He can't stop reliving the past they shared, clinging to memories of joy and love. Eventually, he relocates to a place where they once vacationed together, a place filled with echoes of their happier times.

In this new chapter of his life, Yasha meets Kate, a beautiful, divorced woman whose trust in love was destroyed when her husband betrayed her. Like Yasha, she vowed never to fall in love again.

But fate has other plans.

Through pain and shared sorrow, Yasha and Kate slowly begin to heal each other. Against all odds—and their own resistance—they discover a powerful, unexpected love that gives them both a reason to hope again.

The Call of Evil is a haunting, emotionally rich journey through tragedy, healing, and the enduring power of love.

Zaal

Naser Shahrivar, artist, Screenplay writer, and author of "The Persian Lover, Creed and Greed," is working on his next novel, "Zaal," a Persian classic fantasy adventure. It is a spellbinding story of a young prince whose life of luxury is taken from him at birth. As an infant, he was rescued and raised by a magical bird, Simorgh. Zaal is determined to fight to regain his place in the palace and claim his title. He must find a way to free his newly discovered mother, who is held captive by the king. He faces many obstacles on his journey and can change his fate with the help of his newly found, strong-willed friends. This story is sure to enchant children of all ages.

Zaal will be a self-published book. The author/artist intends to complete a fully illustrated children's book about Zaal.

To order The Persian Lover/Creed and Greed, email:
artandgiftcenter@hotmail.com
Your interest and support are greatly valued.

Dear reader, if you enjoyed reading this book, please leave a review on Amazon Kindle. I read every review and they help new readers to discover my book.